Two weeks, he reminded himself. For O'Halloran Security, he could put up with anything.

Even Abby Porter's smile.

Quinn paused, silently judging the distance between the buildings before cataloging everything else around him. The lodge. The cabins. The boathouse. Even the trees. It gave him an immediate sense of what fit so he would instantly know if something didn't.

So far, the only thing that didn't quite fit was Abby's reaction to him.

She got as tense as a new bowstring if he got too close.

Her bright smile and unexpected sense of humor rose easily to the surface, but several times during the tour Quinn had sensed her retreating within herself. And the flash of panic in her eyes when he'd told her that he planned to stay on-site had bothered him, too. For a split second, she'd seemed…afraid.

Or was he imagining things?

Books by Kathryn Springer

Love Inspired	Steeple Hill
Tested by Fire	*Front Porch Princess*
Her Christmas Wish	*Hearts Evergreen*
By Her Side	*"A Match Made*
For Her Son's Love	*for Christmas"*
A Treasure Worth Keeping	*Picket Fence Promises*
Hidden Treasures	*The Prince Charming List*
Family Treasures	
Jingle Bell Babies	
*A Place to Call Home	

*Mirror Lake

KATHRYN SPRINGER

is a lifelong Wisconsin resident. Growing up in a "newspaper" family, she spent long hours as a child plunking out stories on her mother's typewriter and hasn't stopped writing since! She loves to write inspirational romance because it allows her to combine her faith in God with her love of a happy ending.

A Place to Call Home
Kathryn Springer

Steeple Hill®

Published by Steeple Hill Books™

STEEPLE HILL BOOKS

Steeple Hill®

ISBN-13: 978-0-373-87585-6

A PLACE TO CALL HOME

Copyright © 2010 by Kathryn Springer

www.SteepleHill.com

Printed in U.S.A.

Recycling programs for this product may not exist in your area.

I sought the Lord, and he answered me;
he delivered me from all my fears.
Those who look to him are radiant;
their faces are never covered with shame.

—*Psalms* 34: 4, 5

To Anna

Because I have no doubt there will come a day
when you dedicate a book to me! Remember,
"He who began a good work in you will carry
it on to completion." That's a promise!

Prologue

"Quinn? There's a headache waiting for you on line two."

Ignoring the phone, Quinn O'Halloran shot a wry look at his secretary and reached for the cup of coffee he'd poured over an hour ago instead.

"Mel Burdock," he guessed.

Faye McAllister shook her head. The movement sent the slender gold chains on her bifocals dancing. "No, Burdock's more like the tension headache that climbs up the back of your neck and camps out in your temples. This guy—instant migraine."

"Feel free to correct me on this, but I thought I hired *you* to intercept the migraines."

"You did. But this is the third time today I've intercepted this particular one." Faye aimed a scowl at the phone. "When I told Mr. High and Mighty that your policy is to return phone calls between four and five o'clock, he didn't seem to think it applied to him. He insists on talking directly to you but won't say what he wants. And—" another scowl "—he refused to tell me his name. Must be from out of town."

Quinn suppressed a smile. Faye took pride in her ability to deal with anyone who walked through the door of O'Halloran Security. It was one of the reasons he'd hired her. Quinn preferred to work behind the scenes and let Faye handle the customers. Those she didn't manage to scare away usually ended up signing a contract.

Glancing at the clock, he mentally scrolled through the rest of his afternoon schedule. If he ate lunch in his truck on the way to Mel's, it would give him an extra five minutes to deal with the anonymous headache on the line.

"I'll take it in my office."

"I'm sorry." Faye huffed the words. "If I let a salesman get through, I'll bring in doughnuts tomorrow morning."

Quinn grinned. "Are you kidding? If you let a salesman through, you'll bring in doughnuts for the next month."

After topping off his cup, Quinn followed the worn path down the center of the carpet to the oversize closet in the back of the building that doubled as his office. The red light on his desk phone continued to blink out a warning. A testimony to the caller's patience. Or stubbornness.

With a shake of his head, he picked it up. "O'Halloran."

"It's about time," a voice snapped.

Faye was right. Instant migraine.

"Good morning, Mr.—"

"Alex Porter." There was a significant pause, as if he expected Quinn to recognize the name. "Porter Hotels."

Now Quinn recognized the name.

The deluxe hotels had their roots in Chicago, where Quinn had lived for eight years before returning to Mirror Lake, Wisconsin. Under Alex Porter's management, offshoots now sprouted in other major Midwestern cities. Not only did they successfully compete against the larger, well-known chains, but the fact that Porter Hotels remained a family-run enterprise made it even more unique.

"What can I do for—"

"I want to hire you."

Quinn let out a slow breath. No wonder the guy had raised Faye's hackles. Everything Alex Porter said came out sounding like a command instead of a request. As if he expected his name would open doors that were closed to mere mortals.

The trouble was, Quinn thought with a trace of bitterness, it probably did. He'd dealt with people like Alex Porter before and had no desire to repeat the experience. Unfortunately, he wasn't in a position to turn down business. Any business.

Pride or a paycheck?

Over the past year, while trying to resurrect the business his father had spent the last years of his life determined to bury, Quinn had discovered the cause and effect relationship between the two. Sometimes the first one depended upon the second.

"Are you buying a condo? Building a hotel in the area?" Quinn searched his desk drawer—the Bermuda Triangle of office supplies—for a pen that actually worked. "O'Halloran Security custom designs security systems to fit the needs of each client. We can set up an appointment to discuss the details—"

"I don't need a new security system."

Quinn frowned. "I thought you said you wanted to hire me."

"I do. You recognized my name, and I recognized yours when I was researching businesses in the Mirror Lake area. I don't need an alarm system. This is…personal."

Personal.

Quinn's fingers tightened around the phone. "Sorry. You've got the wrong person."

"I don't think so."

"O'Halloran Security is strictly buildings. I don't provide

personal security." Not anymore. "I'm sorry you wasted your time. But I have an appointment now, so you'll have to excuse me. There are other reputable agencies in the Chicago area. I'm sure you'll find someone."

To walk you to your limo, Quinn added silently.

"It isn't for me. It's for my younger sister."

Something in Porter's voice stopped Quinn from hanging up the phone. A hint of emotion that cracked the surface of the cool, CEO voice. "Just hear me out."

Don't ask.

"Please."

Coming from Porter, the word sounded as if he'd started speaking a foreign language. So, against his better judgment, Quinn asked.

"What's going on?"

"Abby turned in her letter of resignation at the hotel a month ago and bought a run-down lodge a few miles outside of Mirror Lake. She plans to turn it into a bed-and-breakfast." The disapproval leaking into Alex's voice told Quinn how he felt about his sister's decision. "You must have heard about it."

"Maybe." Quinn deliberately kept his voice noncommittal as a conversation he'd overheard stirred in his memory.

Although he tried to keep to himself, he had heard a rumor about the sale of the former Bible camp while waiting for his breakfast one morning at the Grapevine Café, where local gossip brewed as fast as Kate Nichols's industrial-strength coffee.

"So far, Abby refuses to listen to reason and come back to Chicago where she belongs. It looks like I'm going to have to play this her way for a while."

"So why did you call me?" Quinn's lips twisted. "You need a bodyguard to keep the local riffraff away from her?"

That was ironic. At one time, his family portrait would have appeared beside the word *riffraff* in *Webster's Dictionary.*

Alex chose to ignore the sarcasm. "A few weeks ago, someone started harassing me. Vandalized my car. Painted some, shall we say, rather unflattering graffiti on the window of my office. There haven't been any overt threats made, but I want someone to keep an eye on Abby until my private investigator finds out who I angered."

"That could take a while," Quinn said under his breath.

To his amazement, Alex laughed. "It might," he admitted. "I'm not concerned about myself as much as I am about Abby. She is…fragile. I can't believe she's serious about opening a bed-and-breakfast, but it doesn't change the fact that right now she's miles away from civilization, living in a house with hook-and-eye locks on the doors and windows that won't close all the way. I want to be sure she's safe."

Some memories were so bitter he could taste them. "Then you should have done your homework. Because if that's the case, I guarantee you called the wrong person."

A tense silence stretched between them, and Quinn guessed it was because not many people had the guts to point out that Alex Porter made mistakes. Maybe he'd save Quinn the trouble and hang up first.

He didn't.

"You spent four years in the Marine Corps. Seven years with Hamlin Security," Alex recited evenly. "You moved back to your hometown a year ago to take over your father's locksmith business after he died. Since then, you expanded to specialized security systems designed for summer homes and luxury condos."

Apparently Porter *had* done his homework.

All those things were true. But Porter had left out a six-month gap in Quinn's employment history. "You forgot something."

"That you got a raw deal while you worked for Hamlin? Doesn't matter."

Didn't matter?

Under different circumstances, Quinn might have been flattered. Except that he couldn't believe someone could neatly condense the last thirteen years of his life and then dismiss the single event that had ripped it apart. Especially when it had cost him his career—and his reputation.

"I have a business. And it isn't babysitting the rich and famous." *Been there, done that. Still pulling out shrapnel.*

"I need the best. That's you."

"What you need to do is buy your sister a rottweiler and remind her to lock the doors at night," Quinn shot back. "It sounds to me like you're overreacting to a threat that doesn't exist. And even if one does, it's in Illinois, not Wisconsin. She's probably safer here than anywhere."

"I'm not taking any chances when it comes to Abby's safety." A hint of steel sharpened the words. "I want someone with her who's experienced in sensing potential threats."

That was funny. Because Quinn was sensing one right now. A threat to the life he'd started to rebuild.

It was proving to be challenging enough to erase the stain of having the last name O'Halloran without people getting wind of the reason he'd returned to Mirror Lake. Quinn figured if they knew the truth, he'd have to start at square one again. If he was allowed to start at all.

From the sound of it, the only thing Abby Porter was in danger of was being smothered by an overprotective brother. Getting involved with the Porters would be a bad idea, for more reasons than Quinn could count.

"I can't help you."

"You mean you won't help me."

It boiled down to the same thing. "I can give you some names," Quinn offered reluctantly. "Talk to some people I used to know."

Not that he could guarantee those people would talk to him.

"You've heard of the White Wolf Run condominiums, right?" Alex asked. "Jeff Gaines happens to be a close friend of mine."

"Really?" Quinn's voice was stripped of emotion.

Apparently, Porter had not only done his homework, he'd done the extra credit. O'Halloran Security had put in a bid on that job.

A wave of frustration battered Quinn's resolve. This was the difference between the haves and the have-nots. When you belonged to the first group, all you had to do was open your wallet to get your way.

"I can put in a good word for you," Alex said.

The underlying message was clear. If Quinn agreed to work for him.

The confidence in Porter's voice rankled. And brought back that pride versus the paycheck issue again. Designing a security system for the White Wolf Run condos would boost Quinn's income enough to wipe out some of his start-up debt, install an air conditioner in the sweltering office and allow him to replace outdated equipment. It would also go a long way in securing his business's reputation in the area.

And your own.

Quinn ignored the mocking voice that infiltrated his thoughts.

"How does your sister feel about someone invading her personal space?" He wasn't agreeing to anything yet. Just… inquiring.

"It doesn't matter because Abby isn't going to know why you're there. Or that I hired you."

Quinn's internal alarm system went off. "What do you mean she isn't going to know why I'm there?"

"She can't find out that I'm involved in this. We had a bit of a disagreement when she turned in her resignation. Abby refuses to accept any help from me. She can be a little… stubborn."

Apparently a Porter family trait.

"What a shock," Quinn muttered, silently adding that bit of information to what he'd learned about Alex Porter's younger sister so far.

Impulsive. Temperamental. Stubborn—Quinn translated that as *spoiled.* Oh, and what was the other word Alex had used to describe her?

Fragile.

All of them added up to one thing.

Trouble.

"Abby is focused on getting the place ready for her grand opening in August," Alex continued. "Her carpenter, Daniel Redstone, just won an all-expense-paid, two-week vacation with a professional fishing guide. You're going to take his place."

"How lucky for Daniel," Quinn said dryly.

"A person makes their own luck." Alex dismissed his comment. "You've helped Redstone out in the past when you were short on cash. That makes you an obvious replacement for him. No one will think twice about it. Neither will Abby. You'll be able to keep an eye on her and in between pounding nails and painting the outhouse, you can install a security system."

"You are…" Quinn paused. With so many issues to choose from, it was difficult to pick a winner.

"Thorough." Alex filled in the blank.

Quinn had been leaning more toward arrogant. Or smug. But he guessed that description fit as good as any.

"Two weeks. Until Daniel comes back." It was all Quinn was willing to spare. Other than Faye, he only employed two part-time employees. Both men were responsible and would appreciate the extra work, but Quinn didn't want to look as if he were shirking his responsibility. People already told him that he resembled his father. The last thing Quinn wanted to do was act like him.

"Two weeks," Alex agreed. "24/7."

"You have got to be kidding." There was overprotective and then there was downright paranoid.

"That's my offer."

"The person harassing you hasn't bothered your sister." Quinn raked a hand through his hair. "Don't you think that's a little extreme?"

"I told you." Alex's voice was as cold as spring water now. "I'm not taking any chances when it comes to Abby's safety."

"You want me on-site. Round the clock. For two weeks."

"That's right." And before Quinn had a chance to turn him down flat, Alex proceeded to tell him what he would pay for the inconvenience. "Do we have a deal?"

Everything inside Quinn warned him to walk away. But he couldn't. Not if it helped O'Halloran Security succeed.

"We have a deal."

Quinn reminded himself that he'd walked through the fire before. Only this time he had an advantage. He knew how to avoid getting burned.

Chapter One

Abby Porter didn't realize she had company until Mulligan's tail began to thump a welcoming beat against the ground.

Swinging her feet over the side of the chaise longue, she began a hasty search for the sandals she'd kicked off. She'd located one and was in the process of looking for its mate when Mulligan lumbered to his feet.

As the dog trained his gaze on the corner of the house, Abby ignored the shiver that sowed goose bumps up her arms.

Thank you, Alex.

Her older brother's scare tactics were finally getting to her. All part of his plot to get her to come back to Chicago where he could keep a protective eye on her.

"Not a chance," she muttered, tamping down her unease. If she was going to be an innkeeper, she had to get used to people coming and going.

"Who is it, Big Guy? Who's here?"

In response, Mulligan let out a friendly woof. Which told Abby absolutely nothing. The dog's instincts weren't exactly an accurate barometer when it came to assessing a potential threat. A week ago, she'd had to intervene before he got up close and personal with a porcupine during their morning walk around Mirror Lake. Mulligan loved everything, from the squirrels that scolded him from the branches of the oak trees to her reliable, good-natured carpenter Daniel.

Relief swept through her, causing the goose bumps tracking her arms to subside a little, when Abby remembered that Daniel Redstone was supposed to stop by to pick up his paycheck before he left on vacation.

For some reason, he'd expected Abby to be as excited as he was when he'd won an all-expense-paid trip with one of the best professional fishing guides in the state of Wisconsin.

Abby hadn't been excited.

The elderly handyman might have worked at a speed that hovered between slow and a dead standstill, but the final result of his effort was no less than breathtaking. If it hadn't been for Daniel's promise to send over a suitable replacement to fill in for him, Abby would have been tempted to offer a sizeable—but anonymous—donation to the fishing guide's favorite charity if he agreed to cancel the trip.

That the thought had even crossed her mind told Abby that she was already showing some early symptoms of "Alex Porter Syndrome." A disease characterized by an intense desire to control the universe.

In the end, she hadn't had much of a choice but to agree to send Daniel off with her blessing. And consider it another surprise to add to the growing list of surprises she'd encountered since her move to Mirror Lake.

Mulligan's low woof thinned to a whine, and Abby quickly figured out why.

The man rounding the corner of the house wasn't Daniel Redstone.

This man was younger. Much younger. He wasn't stoop-shouldered and thin as a fly rod, either.

Lost tourist?

Abby rejected the thought immediately.

There was nothing *lost* about the man. He moved with the kind of fluid, confident stride she'd always envied. The kind that said he didn't simply *know* his place in the world, he'd carved it out himself. Khaki cargo pants paired with a plain cotton T-shirt accentuated the man's lean, muscular frame but made it difficult to pinpoint what he did for a living.

Abby's eyes narrowed. It would be just like Alex to send one of his minions to keep an eye on her even after she'd told him not to. She loved her brother to pieces but he did have a tendency to bully people to get his way.

She hadn't expected Alex to take the news of her departure well, but she hadn't realized how strongly he would respond to what he labeled her "defection."

A few short months ago, his reaction would have caused her to give in, but this time it had only made her that much more determined to break out on her own. It was time. And the way things had fallen in place, it seemed that God Himself had gone before her to clear the path.

She could only pray that Alex would eventually come around and accept her decision. If Abby were honest with herself—another thing she'd been practicing lately—she had to admit that it was partly her fault that Alex didn't have a lot of confidence in her. For a long time, she hadn't had much confidence in herself.

The stranger spotted her and veered down the uneven brick path leading to the gazebo. As he drew closer, the ruggedly handsome features became more defined. Strands of silky, ink-black hair lay even with the five o'clock shadow darkening his angular jaw. Mirrored sunglasses—Abby had never been a fan—concealed his eyes.

"Hello." Ignoring the second crop of goose bumps that sprouted up her arms, Abby forced a smile. She spotted her flattened sandal in the spot where Mulligan had been dozing and discreetly toed it back on. "Can I help you?"

He stopped several feet away, close enough for her to see her distorted reflection in his sunglasses. "Are you Abby Porter?"

"Yes."

"Then I'm here to help you."

Abby blinked. "Excuse me?"

"I'm Quinn O'Halloran."

The name meant nothing to her. "I'm sorry. I—"

"Daniel Redstone sent me." He yanked off the glasses and Abby found herself staring into a pair of slate gray eyes. "I'm your new carpenter."

"My new..." Abby couldn't push the rest of the sentence past the knot in her throat. She tried again. "He didn't mention you'd be coming over today." Better. The squeak that had made her voice sound like a rusty screen door was barely noticeable now.

He shrugged. "According to Daniel, you're under a tight deadline and need to keep the project moving along. I thought I'd stop by and take a look around to get a feel for things before I start."

"I am under a deadline but— Mulligan, no!" Abby lunged for the dog, who'd finally summoned the courage to inch close enough to swipe his tongue against Quinn's hand. She gave him an apologetic smile. "I'm sorry. We're still working on basic etiquette."

"You're a golfer."

"Golf?" At first the meaning behind his statement didn't

sink in. When it did, Abby smiled. "No, I borrowed the term because I adopted Mulligan from the animal shelter an hour before he was to be euthanized."

"Another chance." The pale gray eyes lit with sudden understanding.

"It seemed to fit." Abby ruffled one of Mulligan's floppy ears. "And I happen to think everyone deserves a second one, don't you?"

Quinn didn't answer. Because Abby Porter's megawatt smile had momentarily short-circuited the hardware in his brain.

He knew her.

No, Quinn silently corrected the thought. He'd seen her before. On billboards strategically placed around the city of Chicago. Wearing black velvet and pearls. The reigning princess of Porter Hotels.

Only this princess looked different. And not only because of her smile. Honey-blond hair, caught in a casual knot at the base of her neck, accentuated delicate features dominated by a pair of eyes that were silver-green like an aspen leaf.

Instead of black velvet, she wore figure-hugging jeans, a paint-splattered T-shirt and a pair of sandals decorated with the gaudiest plastic daisies he'd ever seen.

But looks could be deceiving. He'd learned that the hard way. As far as Quinn was concerned, a diva in blue jeans was still a diva. Before she'd been aware of his arrival, he'd caught a glimpse of her reclining on the chaise longue with a book propped in her lap. Obviously she was so motivated to get the inn ready for her grand opening that she was taking a break before the day had barely started.

Quinn steeled himself against her smile, unnerved that it had had such an effect on him.

"Do you think you can spare a few minutes to give me a tour of the place?" He leveled a pointed gaze at the chaise longue.

"Of course." Abby's smile faded.

Quinn wasn't quite prepared for the direct hit to his conscience. If he'd forgotten the reason he'd changed his professional focus from providing security to buildings instead of people, a few seconds in Abby Porter's company had brought it crashing back. Buildings were easy to figure out. People, not so much.

They fell into step together, and Abby switched into tour guide mode.

"The main lodge started out as a private vacation retreat for a wealthy family, but eventually they donated it to a local church." She gestured toward the sprawling two-story split-log home that Quinn had passed on his way to the gazebo. "The congregation built five additional cabins on the water and turned it into a retreat center and Bible camp. Eventually, though, they couldn't keep up with the larger, more modern camps and had to turn it over to the bank."

Quinn could empathize. He knew all too well what it felt like to struggle to keep a business afloat.

"After that," Abby went on, "it ended up in the hands of a developer. He planned to replace the lodge with condos but later realized it wouldn't appeal to tourists who wanted a full recreation lake…and easier access to civilization. Most of the people who come back to Mirror Lake think of it as a second home rather than a vacation spot. They appreciate the slower pace."

"That's why you chose to turn the place into a bed-and-breakfast rather than a resort," Quinn guessed. "It will attract the type of clientele looking for peace and quiet."

Abby gave him an approving look. "It sat empty for almost

five years until my Realtor happened to mention it a few months after I started looking. Believe it or not, I had to beg her to show it to me." Her voice dropped to a whisper. "But the first time I saw it, I knew it was perfect."

Quinn looked over at the lake, as clear and smooth as window glass, beyond a stand of towering white pines. He'd moved to Chicago after his tour of duty because he'd been ready to take on the world. Ready for a fresh start where no one knew the name O'Halloran. The energy and pace of the city had matched his lifestyle. Or so he'd thought. Until he moved back to Mirror Lake.

That first night Quinn spent in his childhood home, temperatures had dipped into the forties, but he'd crawled out the window of his old bedroom and sat on the roof.

He'd forgotten what it felt like to see the stars at night. To drive for miles without seeing a single house or apartment complex. Quinn may not have wanted to return to the town where he'd grown up but he hadn't expected to feel a tug on his soul, as if he were still connected to it. Especially when his memories of the place weren't exactly the Hallmark kind.

Sensing that Abby was waiting for a response, Quinn's gaze moved from the lodge to the weathered cabins strung like wooden beads along the shoreline. Work, work and more work. But he was reluctant to strip the sparkle from Abby's eyes. Again.

"It's got potential," he heard himself say.

Abby turned and smiled up at him. "I think so, too."

Once again, Quinn wasn't prepared for the force of Abby's smile.

Focus, O'Halloran.

"What time does the rest of the crew usually get here?"

Abby shot him a puzzled look. "The rest of the crew?"

"The *work* crew," Quinn clarified.

Abby's low laugh went straight through him. "Now that Daniel is gone, you're looking at it."

She couldn't be serious. "You and Daniel have been doing everything yourselves?"

"That's right." Abby reached down to fondle Mulligan's ears. "I hired some teenagers to do some painting, but they have other jobs so they're only available on the weekend." She skipped up the wide plank steps and opened the front door. "I moved in at the beginning of June and started working on the main house right away. It was in fair condition but I'm still in the process of…"

The rest of the words dissolved in Quinn's ears as he stepped through the doorway into the great room.

The place was a wreck.

Fair condition, Abby had said. The grand opening was a month away but Quinn saw three months of hard labor. At least.

No wonder her Realtor had tried to discourage her from purchasing the property and her brother had had a fit.

Quinn didn't have to be a professional carpenter to see that the hardwood floors needed to be varnished, the walls painted and another coat of stain applied to the tongue-and-groove pine ceiling.

Abby tilted her head and a strand of sun-streaked blond hair molded itself to the curve of her cheek. "So, what do you think?"

"Wow." That about covered it.

Abby grinned. "I'll show you the kitchen."

Can't wait, Quinn thought.

He followed her, silently adding projects to the list with every step. New baseboards. New trim. New light fixtures.

It didn't make sense. Abby Porter was an heiress. She had

the resources to level the entire place and have it rebuilt in a week. So why was she doing the bulk of the work herself?

"The kitchen is original to the lodge when it was built in the 1940s, so it has a lot of vintage charm." Abby paused in the doorway.

Vintage charm. A Realtor's term for gold linoleum and chrome-trimmed Formica countertops.

He stepped past her, bracing himself for what was behind door number one.

"Your eyes are closed," Abby said.

So they were. Quinn opened them. "They're adjusting to the change in light."

He had to look. No getting around it.

Relief crashed over him when he stepped into a room that could have been featured in a home decorating magazine. Given the fact the place was going to be a bed-and-breakfast, it shouldn't have come as a surprise that Abby had devoted most of her time and effort to the kitchen.

She'd stayed true to the time period by keeping the original glass-front cupboards and painting the bead board walls a sunny shade of yellow. Old-fashioned dish towels had been recycled into valances.

The marble-topped island in the center of the kitchen blended seamlessly with the vintage decor but the granite sink and gleaming stainless steel appliances were definitely modern, state-of-the-art tools for the serious cook.

Quinn's gaze continued around the room and snagged on an ancient green oven, straight off the set of a seventies sitcom.

"I couldn't part with her." Abby followed the direction of his eyes and accurately read his expression. "She's an icon."

"She?"

"Mrs. Avocado."

She'd *named* the oven. "Does she...*it*...still work?"

"Sometimes."

"Correct me if I'm wrong, but if you're running a bed-and-breakfast, don't you need an oven that works *all* the time?"

"She's a little temperamental but we're getting to know each other." Abby gave the appliance an affectionate pat.

Quinn steeled himself against the woman's infectious charm. Abby Porter was a *job*. He didn't want to think of her as a person. And he certainly didn't want to *like* her.

Maybe Faye didn't need a new air conditioner in the office that badly....

Unaware of his thoughts, Abby tapped the toe of one sandal on the ceramic tile beneath their feet, setting the plastic petals into motion. "The floor was a bit of a challenge because it wasn't even when I started."

"You did all this yourself?"

Abby's shoulders lifted in a modest shrug. "It wasn't that hard. I bought a book."

She'd bought a book.

"Are you ready to see the rest?" Abby was already on her way out the door. "I hate to rush the tour but I still have a hundred things to do today."

"More like a million," Quinn muttered.

"Excuse me?" Abby paused on her way out the door.

"Nothing. Lead on."

While Abby took him through the rest of the house, Quinn followed along, taking mental notes along the way. Alex, he discovered, hadn't been exaggerating. The windows on the first floor were the old-fashioned casement kind that had gone the way of the eight-track tape player. And a chimpanzee with a nail file could have picked the locks on the doors.

Abby wanted him working on the cabins but Quinn knew

he'd have to come up with a plan that would put him along-side Abby at the lodge in order to make the house secure.

"This bedroom is called Serenity." Abby paused to open one of the doors. "I finished painting the trim this morning."

"This morning?" Quinn raised an eyebrow. He'd pulled in to the driveway at nine. "What time this morning?"

Abby tucked her full lower lip between her teeth before answering the question. "Mmm. I think it was around four."

"Four o'clock in the *morning?*"

One slim shoulder lifted. "And some people think insomnia is a bad thing."

Quinn didn't comment because he was trying to wrap his mind around the fact that Abby had been up before dawn. Working. He could relate. He'd done the same thing after he'd moved back to Mirror Lake. Slept a little, worked a lot. Especially because his father, in his final months, hadn't bothered to put money into anything other than the cash register at the local liquor store.

"So what do you think? Does it live up to its name?"

Abby's question yanked him back from the edge of those memories and he looked past her into the bedroom.

Quinn had expected Abby to copy the more popular rustic decor—characterized by an overabundance of largemouth bass and whitetail deer—used in other places that catered to tourists.

Instead, by combining cool blues and soft greens, Abby had brought the outdoors inside. And in the process, provided a comfortable oasis guaranteed to instantly lower a person's blood pressure.

"Very serene." Quinn's own blood pressure didn't agree with the assessment. Not with Abby standing close enough that he caught the faintest whiff of…*cinnamon?*…in the air.

Not exactly a designer fragrance but oddly appealing. "Where is your room?" he asked abruptly.

Abby blinked. "On the third floor. I didn't want to take up space the guests could use. Plus, there's an enclosed, private staircase leading up to it, so I have my own entrance."

"There's a third floor?" Considering the two levels of windows on the house, Quinn wouldn't have guessed the house had an additional story.

"It's more like an attic, really, but if you don't count the cabins, I have the best view of the lake."

Quinn debated whether he should ask her to prove it but decided to wait for another time. When Abby was occupied with something else he'd take a look at it.

"Speaking of the cabins, maybe you should show me the one I'll be staying in so I can start unloading some of my things."

"The cabin you'll be staying in?" Abby echoed. "What do you mean?"

"I'll be living on-site until Daniel gets back. Didn't he mention that?"

"No." Abby's eyes darkened with an emotion Quinn couldn't quite identify. "As a matter of fact, he didn't."

Chapter Two

"Is there a problem?"

Definitely more than one, Abby thought as she tried to tamp down her rising panic.

She might have been rambling on like a cruise director who'd downed a shot of espresso, but she thought she'd done a pretty good job hiding her emotions after Quinn O'Halloran introduced himself as the new carpenter. But once again the man had thrown her completely off balance.

"You can't stay…*here.* I don't know what Daniel was thinking if he told you differently."

"Why not?" Quinn leaned against the door frame and tucked his hands into the front pockets of his jeans.

Why not?

Abby wasn't sure how to respond to the question. Was she being silly? Or worse yet, paranoid? Daniel had assured her that the carpenter he was sending over had worked with him before and came with excellent references. But having Quinn O'Halloran working on the property and having him *living* on the property were two different things entirely.

Over the past month, she and Daniel had settled into a pleasant routine. Abby concentrated on renovations in the main lodge while he tackled the cabins. During their lunch break, Abby coaxed Daniel to sample the results of a new recipe while the elderly carpenter entertained her with stories about small town life. His off-key whistle provided comforting background music in the late afternoon when Abby moved outside to weed the flowerbeds.

She couldn't shake the feeling that Quinn's presence wouldn't be quite so comforting.

"You must have a place of your own," she stammered.

"I live a few miles north of town, so I would have a half hour's commute every day," Quinn said. "Look at it this way—I can put in longer days if I'm staying on-site. Shave some time off the project. Nothing against Daniel, but I work a little faster than he does."

"I don't—"

"And I could use the hours."

Abby's protest died in her throat. Quinn's voice had remained neutral but the subtle tightening of his jaw told her the admission had cost him. She felt a stab of guilt, knowing her hesitance had forced him to confess that he needed the extra income.

She could pay his mileage…

Just as she opened her mouth to make the offer, another thought pushed its way in.

Was it possible that Quinn was, in a roundabout way, an answer to her prayers? The grand opening was scheduled for the beginning of August but even Daniel had been skeptical they'd make the deadline. Abby planned to focus her attention for the next few weeks on the great room but several of the cabins still needed work. If Quinn finished remodeling them, she could be at capacity opening weekend.

Just because God hadn't answered her prayer in the way she expected didn't mean that He hadn't answered it.

Okay, God, I'm going to assume Your hand is in this.

Abby forced a smile. "You might be ready to escape at the end of the day once you see what kind of shape the cabins are in."

"I'll stay until the job is finished." Quinn's eyes met hers. "You can count on it."

Abby's heart did a curious little flip and she backed away from that quicksilver gaze. Realizing her hands were clenched into fists at her side, she forced herself to relax.

Daniel, she reminded herself, was the closest thing she had to a friend in Mirror Lake. He wouldn't have asked Quinn to take his place if he didn't trust him. And with the grand opening looming, Daniel probably thought he'd done her a favor by suggesting that Quinn live on the grounds.

She released the breath she hadn't realized she'd been holding. "Two of the cabins are finished so you can take your pick. Both have kitchenettes and full baths…"

The cell phone in her pocket interrupted, playing the dramatic opening notes of Beethoven's *Symphony No. 5*. A special ring tone for a bossy big brother.

Abby took it out of her pocket but instead of answering it, she shut off the sound.

"I don't mind if you take a call," Quinn said.

"That's all right. I don't mind ignoring this one." Abby released a sigh. "My brother calls at least once a day to ask if I've come to my senses yet."

"Come to your senses?"

"He's a little overprotective." An understatement, but at the moment Abby couldn't come up with a better description. "He's part of the reason I bought this place. I love my brother but he doesn't understand that God might have a different plan for my life than the one *he* thinks I should follow."

God.

The comfortable way she said the word made Quinn…uncomfortable. Sure, he believed that God existed, but if the people living in Mirror Lake were reluctant to give an O'Halloran a second chance, Quinn didn't expect that God would, either. Especially when they'd parted company long ago.

"What does your brother think you should do?" he asked.

"Give in," Abby muttered under her breath.

Quinn raised a questioning brow.

"We have a…family business and he wanted me to stay there." A fascinating blush of pink tinted her ivory cheeks.

Interesting. Abby seemed reluctant to let him know just what that family business revolved around.

It seemed they both had their secrets.

"You didn't like it," Quinn prompted.

"I didn't say that."

He frowned. "Then why—"

Abby's phone rang again. Quinn gave her points for her sense of humor. It couldn't be a coincidence that the ominous opening notes from one of Beethoven's most famous symphonies warned of an incoming call from Alex.

"Did I say overprotective?" Abby rolled her eyes. "I meant overbearing. And persistent. Which means I should probably get this over with or he'll keep calling."

And calling and calling, Quinn wanted to add. The normally unflappable Faye McAllister was still suffering from post-traumatic Porter syndrome. "Not a problem. I'll meet you down by the cabins."

"Thank you." Abby's bright smile surfaced. And lingered in his memory as Quinn left the room.

"Hi, Big Brother," he heard her say. "And yes, you can take that in the George Orwell *1984* way that I intended it."

As the screen door snapped shut behind him, a smile pulled at the corner of Quinn's lips.

Alex had mentioned that he and Abby had had a falling-out when she'd left Chicago, but Quinn didn't miss the exasperated affection in Abby's tone when she'd described her brother. And Alex's frustration over her decision to move to Mirror Lake hadn't overridden his desire to look out for her, no matter how stubborn he thought she was being.

They cared about each other.

Quinn ignored a pinch of envy. That kind of family loyalty was foreign to him.

Stepping onto the deck, he almost tripped over Mulligan, asleep in a pool of sunshine. He shook his head. Abby could have chosen a more protective breed, especially given the isolated location of the inn.

Abby thought everyone deserved a second chance.

If Abby Porter lived in the real world instead of an ivory tower, she'd realize that most people didn't share her view.

Mulligan rolled to his feet and trotted after Quinn as he crossed the lawn toward the cabins.

Home, sweet home. For the next two weeks.

Even though he'd agreed to Alex's terms, Quinn planned to play by his own set of rules. That meant he would satisfy the job requirements by being close enough to see the main house and yet be able to keep an eye on whoever was coming and going.

And on Abby.

The ease with which he shifted back into his former role surprised him a little. A little over a year ago, he'd emptied his locker at Hamlin Security, nodded to the former colleague who'd walked him out of the building and drove away without a backward glance.

Until Alex Porter had temporarily forced him back into the business.

Two weeks, he reminded himself. For O'Halloran Security, he could put up with anything.

Even Abby Porter's smile.

Quinn paused, silently judging the distance between the buildings before cataloging everything else around him. The lodge. The cabins. The boathouse. Even the trees. It gave him an immediate sense of what fit so he would instantly know if something didn't.

So far, the only thing that didn't quite fit was Abby's reaction to *him*.

She got as tense as a new bowstring if he got too close.

Her bright smile and unexpected sense of humor rose easily to the surface but several times during the tour Quinn had sensed her retreating within herself. And the flash of panic in her eyes when he'd told her that he planned to stay on-site had bothered him, too. For a split second, she'd seemed…afraid.

Or he was imagining things?

At one point, Quinn had trusted his instincts about people. Not anymore. A six-month assignment working for the Raynes family had cured him of that.

Forcing thoughts of Abby aside for the moment, Quinn walked toward the cedar-sided cabin positioned closest to the house. The one with an unobstructed view of the driveway.

His foot touched the first step. And went right through it.

Perfect.

Quinn tugged his shoe free and continued the inspection. The wooden screen door sagged on its hinges and it looked as if a family of chipmunks had taken up residence in the fireplace.

He was prowling around the tiny kitchen when he heard Abby's breathless voice. "Are you in here?"

"Yup."

When Abby appeared in the doorway, her cheeks were flushed. Quinn wasn't sure if it was from a run-in with Alex or because she'd run all the way from the house. No matter what the reason, she looked way too fetching for his peace of mind.

Quinn turned his attention to the fieldstone fireplace instead.

That's right. Because you'll really be effective looking out for Abby when you can't even look at her.

"You'll probably want to move into North Star Cabin," Abby said. "Daniel finished it last week."

Quinn had seen the sign over the door of that particular cabin and it sat on a curve of shoreline, surrounded on three sides by a fortress of mature trees. "This one will be fine."

Abby's eyes widened. "The windows are broken and the screens need to be replaced."

"So?"

She laughed. *Laughed.* "Are you kidding? The mosquitoes will treat you like an all-you-can-eat buffet if you sleep in here."

"I'll install the windows this afternoon, then. I figure if I stayed in one of the cabins that needed remodeling, I'll be motivated to get it done faster."

Indecision skimmed through Abby's eyes. He'd used the magic word again. *Faster.* The pressure to be ready in time for the grand opening would convince her to let him have his way.

Her lips compressed. "I can't let you stay here, Mr. O'Halloran."

Or not.

"It's Quinn."

"Quinn." The color in her cheeks deepened. "What if it rains? The roof leaks."

He could tell she was wavering.

"Clear skies predicted through the weekend. And I'll replace the shingles on the roof after the new windows are in."

"The new furniture is on back order. You'd have to sleep on the couch and it's not very comfortable."

Tell that to the chipmunks, Quinn thought. They seemed to be pretty comfortable there. "I've slept in worse conditions, believe me."

The indecision on Abby's face changed to curiosity, and Quinn mentally kicked himself. The less she knew about him the better. Granted, if she wanted to get an earful about the O'Halloran family history, all she had to do was ask some of the old-timers in town. But as far as Quinn knew, no one, not even Faye, knew what had happened while he'd been employed at Hamlin.

He planned to keep it that way. It was difficult enough to erase the stain from the name O'Halloran without bringing up the reason he'd returned to Mirror Lake after a fifteen-year absence.

"Fine." Abby finally gave in. "I'll make sure you have fresh linens. When will you be…moving in?"

"Today."

"Today?" Abby's arms locked around her stomach in a protective gesture that set off warning bells in Quinn's head.

"If that's all right with you," he added, watching her body language.

Abby's arms dropped to her sides but her fists remained clenched. "I suppose so."

On a hunch, Quinn took a few steps back and propped a hip against the antique trestle table in the center of the room. Abby's shoulders relaxed but the wary look in her eyes lingered.

Was she *afraid* of him? Or had she gotten skittish because her brother provided daily updates on the person harassing him, in an attempt to convince her to come home? Both possibilities left a bad taste in Quinn's mouth.

"Where did Daniel leave the tools?" Quinn hoped the subtle reminder that he was going to get to work right away would put the light back in her face.

It did. But not as quickly as he'd hoped.

"He didn't leave anything here. He probably assumed you'd use your own."

"Right." Because any self-respecting carpenter would use his own tools.

He'd have to stop in at the hardware store and pick up some new ones. And send Alex Porter the bill.

Chapter Three

Abby spent the rest of the afternoon in the kitchen, perfecting a recipe for the baking powder biscuits she planned to use to make strawberry shortcake that evening.

Some people escaped to the gym or a spa when their stress levels went off the charts. Abby escaped to the kitchen. Until she'd become friends with Jessica Benson, who'd joined the staff as a pastry chef at Porter Lakeside the previous winter, she hadn't looked at herself as anything more than a dabbler in the culinary arts.

Jessica was the one who'd dared her one evening to serve her chocolate mousse crepes with raspberry vanilla sauce to the hotel guests rather than the appreciative wait staff that usually reaped the rewards of Abby's stressful day.

They'd been such a hit that Jessica had included them on the dessert menu. The next day, she'd asked Abby why she was wasting her talents, doing what was expected of her, rather than being in the kitchen doing what she loved.

Once Abby had gotten over her initial defensiveness, they had become the best of friends. Not only had Jessica encouraged her not to settle on the path of least resistance, she'd been instrumental in bringing Abby to a crossroads where she'd made the most important decision of her life. To surrender her heart to God and follow Him. No matter where He led her.

And Abby was convinced, in spite of her fears and the occasional setback, that He'd led her to Mirror Lake.

She tipped her face toward the ceiling.

Thank You, Lord.

She felt as if she'd been repeating those three simple words over and over, but nothing else seemed to fit. She *was* thankful.

Don't hold on to your fears, Jessica had told her the day she'd left. *Hold on to God instead.*

Sometimes that was easier said than done, but Abby was trying. While Jessica had sent her off with a hug and words of encouragement, Alex had lectured her. Warned her that sharing her home with the guests was a far cry from simply handing them a keycard and leaving them to their own devices. *No privacy,* he'd told her. *Your life won't be your own.*

If Abby hadn't understood the underlying reason for the warning, she might have been tempted to tell him that her life had never felt like her own anyway. But after she'd turned it over to the Lord, the excitement over what He planned to do with it overrode her fears. Most of the time.

Lost in thought, Abby stared down at the bowl of ingredients, wondering if she'd added the right amount of flour. With a sigh, she dumped it back into the canister and began to measure it out again.

This time, she couldn't hold Alex responsible for the dozens of biscuits cooling on wire racks around the kitchen. Or the reason she was so distracted today. This time, her new carpenter was to blame.

Quinn O'Halloran.

She'd seen him mask his dismay when he'd walked into the lodge that morning. Not that she could blame him. There was a lot of work left to accomplish.

The to-do list taped to the refrigerator filled one side of a piece of paper and half the other. Daniel's absence had already put her behind schedule. Which was the reason she'd agreed, against her better judgment, to let Quinn stay in one of the cabins.

As long as the cabins were ready for the grand opening, everything else would work out. Abby had discovered she wasn't ready to put guests in the main house right away. Years of having her privacy fiercely guarded had seeped into her personality in ways she hadn't acknowledged until she'd moved out from under the protection of her family's last name.

The rhythmic tap of a hammer paused for a moment and Abby couldn't resist peeking out the window. Quinn had left after she'd shown him the rest of the cabins but returned a few hours later and went straight to work. True to his word, he'd started with the cabin windows. Most of the building materials had been delivered before Abby arrived in Mirror Lake and she'd shown Quinn the musty garage where everything was stored.

His progress—and that, she told herself sternly, was what she was checking on—gave her a renewed hope that she would be open for business right on schedule.

Something moved near Quinn's feet and even from the distance separating them, Abby knew what it was. Mulligan. He'd whined at the door when Quinn's truck had returned, preferring to nap in the great outdoors at the new carpenter's feet than with her in the sunlit kitchen.

The traitor.

After removing the last batch of biscuits from the oven, Abby cleaned up the kitchen and then slipped out the back door, where she'd hung a load of sheets and towels on the line.

On warm afternoons, she preferred to put the sun to work instead of the industrial-sized dryer in the utility room. The Porter Hotels' housekeeping staff would have shaken their heads at the extra work but Abby found pleasure in doing things the old-fashioned way.

As she approached the cabin where Quinn was working, two dogs streaked toward her. Mulligan barked several times, as if introducing her to the lively, buff-colored cocker spaniel that bounced at his side as if it had springs in its paws.

Abby braced herself for impact but the dog pulled up short at the last second and sat down, lifting one dainty paw for her to shake.

Charmed, Abby set the laundry basket down and dropped to her knees. "Aren't you a little sweetheart? What's your name?"

"Abby, Lady. Lady, Abby." Quinn sauntered over, pushing the hammer into the leather tool belt that rode low on his narrow hips. He'd swapped the khaki pants he'd been wearing that morning for a pair of well-worn jeans. "We're roommates, so I had to bring her along."

Which meant that other than Lady, Quinn lived alone. For some reason Abby's heart—totally on its own accord—lifted and performed a brief pirouette at the thought.

"I know what you're thinking."

Abby sincerely hoped that wasn't true. "I wasn't thinking anything. But now that you mention it, Lady is…"

"She's what?" Quinn's eyes narrowed, as if he'd heard it before.

Not the type of dog Abby would have pictured riding shotgun in Quinn's pickup.

"Beautiful." Abby smiled as the spaniel tried to squirm into her lap. "Mulligan will love having company. If you ask him, I think he'd tell you that I'm pretty boring."

* * *

Not with that smile.

Quinn slapped the thought away as soon as it surfaced.

Apparently his former life wasn't as ingrained as he'd thought. Because he'd broken one of the cardinal rules of the trade. Don't get personally involved with a client.

You tried that once, remember? Look where it got you.

Frustration surged through him. Because nothing, beginning with his first glimpse of Abby Porter, had gone the way he'd expected.

First, he got another earful from Faye when he'd stopped by the office on his way through town. Even though the appointment book had a lot of white space, she'd been suspicious from the moment Quinn had informed her that he would be temporarily filling in for Daniel Redstone. He shouldn't have been surprised. Faye scolded him often enough about his tendency to micromanage the business, so his sudden decision to turn O'Halloran Security over to his part-time employees for two weeks had been out of character. The promise of a new air conditioner had finally appeased her, and he'd managed to escape.

Conscious of the time, Quinn had driven home, tossed some of his possessions into the back of the truck and boosted an ecstatic Lady into the passenger seat.

On the way back to the lodge, Alex had called him. Twice, because Quinn had ignored the phone the first time. He wanted to know why Quinn wasn't with Abby. He wanted to know how work on the inn was progressing. And he wanted Quinn to give him updates—*daily updates*—on how his sister seemed to be handling the stress.

The last request had given Quinn the opportunity to educate Alex on the difference between providing personal security and spying. Porter hadn't been happy with the lesson but Quinn knew he had to draw the line somewhere. Plus, Alex's attitude toward Abby had rubbed Quinn the wrong way. It was true she didn't seem like the type to take on a project as large as renovating an old former Bible camp but something in the determined set of Abby's chin made Quinn wonder if she wasn't up to the challenge.

Quinn had been tempted to tell Porter that, too, except he didn't know how to say it without sounding as if he were getting emotionally involved. And because he didn't *do* emotionally involved anymore, he'd simply cut the conversation short and decided he'd be screening his calls from now on.

There'd been no sign of Abby when he parked the truck in the driveway, but he'd heard her singing along with the music filtering through the open windows. Relief had poured through him. If Abby was inside, it meant that he could be outside. And Quinn welcomed the chance to clear his head.

It had worked. Up until the moment he spotted Abby walking across the yard, a laundry basket anchored against one hip. The sight of her felt like another kick to his solar plexus.

If possible, she looked even prettier than she had that morning.

Quinn tried not to notice the way the sunlight picked out the gold and platinum highlights in her hair. Or how the bright pink apron, fashioned to look like a slice of watermelon, accentuated her slender waist and the gentle curve of her hips.

"Have you had Lady since she was a puppy?" Abby asked, unaware that her smile scraped like sandpaper against Quinn's already frayed nerves.

"I inherited her."

"Inherited her?"

"My dad passed away last year. Lady belonged to him." Quinn didn't bother to add that the dog had been another innocent victim of his father's neglect. The day before the funeral, Quinn had followed a rusty chain anchored around the post of the deck to a box made of scrap wood underneath an oak tree in the backyard. He knelt down to look inside and was stunned to see a pair of bright but wary eyes staring back at him.

Quinn hadn't known his father even owned a dog but it didn't surprise him a bit that he hadn't taken care of it. Mike O'Halloran's legacy was one of abuse and neglect. He'd let his family splinter apart, his house practically fall down around his ears and his locksmith business slide to the verge of bankruptcy.

While Quinn debated whether he should try and lure the dog out or simply call animal control, Lady had taken charge of the situation. She'd sidled up to him, her coat matted and dirty, and politely lifted a paw for him to shake.

Quinn had picked her up, taken her into the house and fed her. Then he gave her a bath. That night, Lady staked a claim near his feet when he went to bed.

She'd been there ever since.

"I'm sorry about your father." Abby rose to her feet and laid her hand on Quinn's arm. It took all his self-control not to jerk away from her touch. "My parents died when I was fourteen. They were flying home from a convention in a friend's twin-engine plane. There was some sort of mechanical failure…" Her voice trailed off, the memory—and the pain—as fresh in her eyes as if it had happened only the week before.

"You mentioned a brother. Alex. Do you have other siblings?" Quinn thrust his hands in his pockets, jostling her hand from his arm.

A heartbeat of silence preceded her answer. "No. Just Alex. He's eight years older than I am. He was finishing his last semester of college but he came home and took over the… I mean—" Abby caught herself. "He kept things going."

Took over, Quinn thought wryly, was probably a more accurate description. Still, he couldn't imagine the kind of pressure Alex Porter had faced after the death of their parents. Not only had he stepped into his father's shoes as CEO of Porter Hotels, he'd become an instant guardian to a much younger sibling. It went a long way in explaining why he was so protective of Abby.

Their eyes met and she backpedaled, almost tripping over the laundry basket in the process. "I'll put these sheets and towels inside the cabin for you."

Quinn released a sigh as the two dogs bounded after her. When he followed a few minutes later, he found Abby in the kitchen, eyeing the meager bag of groceries he'd dumped in the middle of the kitchen table.

"You brought…food."

"I don't expect you to provide my meals."

Abby's teeth tucked into her lower lip, a habit that Quinn had noticed seemed to coincide with her desire to say something she wasn't sure she should. The trait must have slipped through the cracks of the Porter DNA. Alex had no trouble saying what was on his mind.

"I know, but…" She picked up a can of ravioli and it looked to Quinn as if she shuddered. "It's silly to cook for myself when I can easily make enough for two."

Sharing meals with Abby. Quinn stifled a groan. Granted, it meant more time in her company but it also meant…more time in her company.

He scooped up a few cans of tuna and shoved them in the cupboard. "That isn't necessary. I'll make do."

"I've been trying out different recipes to serve to the guests." Abby paused to study the label on a loaf of white bread. "Daniel was my official food critic. And since you're taking his place as my carpenter, you might as well take his place as the taste tester, too."

The offer was reasonable. And generous. At the moment, Quinn wasn't sure he was in the mood to be either. He didn't *want* to get to know Abby better. "Thanks, but I'll get more done if I work at my own pace and don't have to stop for meals at certain times."

I'll get more done. He'd said the words deliberately but Abby didn't react the way he'd expected. Instead, she stared at him thoughtfully, as if he were a chessboard and she was studying her next move.

"Mmm." That was all she said. But instead of leaving, Abby began to sort through the groceries and put them away. Quinn joined in, only to speed up the process so he could get back to work. And put some distance between them again.

She clucked her tongue with something that sounded like disapproval.

Quinn slanted a look at Abby and caught her frowning at the can of soup in her hand. "What's wrong? Is it expired?"

"It's chicken noodle."

"So?"

"If you put chicken and water and some noodles into a pot, it turns into chicken noodle soup. Homemade. Which means it tastes better."

"That takes time."

"So?"

Quinn resisted the urge to smile when Abby tossed the word back at him. "So I work a lot. It's easier to open a can."

Both were the truth. He didn't work full-time as a carpenter, which was what Abby assumed he did for a living, but the long hours spent rebuilding O'Halloran Security called for sacrifices in other areas. Like his entire life. But that didn't appear to matter. Abby rolled her eyes and put it in the cupboard next to a box of generic macaroni and cheese.

"Macaroni. Cheese. This isn't hard to make, either," she muttered.

"Really?" Quinn raised an eyebrow. "Because I would think it's extremely challenging to locate fluorescent orange cheese, grind it into a powder and seal it in a tiny foil package."

Abby laughed. The lilting sound poured through the tiny kitchen. And swept right through his defenses. Fortunately, Abby's cell phone chirped, granting him a few moments to shore them up again.

"I'm sorry." She glanced at the number and a shadow skimmed through her eyes. "I should take this."

"No problem." Quinn retreated to the cabin deck and picked up one of the windows. Through the screen, he could hear one side of the conversation.

"I don't care and I don't think my attorney will, either." A long silence followed before Abby spoke again, her tone glacial. "Did he mention that Abby Porter is the one who called? No? Well, you might want to mention my name…yes. Thank you."

Quinn's lips twisted.

He'd never have put that autocratic, hand-me-my-crown-and-scepter voice with the woman in the paint-splattered T-shirt who'd offered to make him dinner.

What's the matter? You expected to see this side of her.

That was true. But he hadn't expected to be so disappointed.

Chapter Four

❧

"In other words, the Lord is giving you another opportunity to trust Him. And to grow."

Abby sighed, knowing her friend was right. Jessica always had a wonderful way of cutting to the heart of an issue and letting God's light shine through the cracks.

"With all the opportunities He's been giving me lately, I should be growing as fast as Jack's beanstalk," Abby grumbled good-naturedly.

Jessica chuckled. "No one said opening a bed-and-breakfast would be easy. But do you still think it's worth it?"

"Yes." Abby didn't hesitate.

"There you go, then." Jessica's smile was evident in her voice. "So, what happened today that made you doubt it? Another pleasant phone call from Alexander the Great?"

Abby choked. *"Jessica."*

"Sorry. Did I say that with a lack of proper reverence? I didn't mean to."

She had and they both knew it. Abby grinned. "I'm surprised Alex didn't fire you after I left. He suspects you were the one who put the idea of a bed-and-breakfast into my head, you know."

"But if he fires me he'll also lose one of his best managers. Who, by the way, happens to be my loving—and very loyal—husband."

"You're right about that."

Alex, for all his controlling ways, depended on Tony Benson to keep the cogs in all four hotels running smoothly. If he ever decided to leave, Abby knew that her brother would feel as if he were missing his right arm.

"Of course I am," Jessica said smugly. "So if I can't blame Alex, what was the challenge of the day?"

An image of Quinn's face flashed in Abby's mind before she could prevent it.

"I told you that Daniel Redstone won a vacation and took two weeks off, right?" Abby plucked a wooden spoon out of a ceramic crock on the counter. "His replacement showed up this morning."

"And you don't think he's going to work out?"

Abby hesitated. So far, she couldn't complain about Quinn's work ethic. The last time she looked outside, he'd already moved to the windows on the other side of the cabin.

Out of sight but definitely not out of mind.

"I'm sure he'll work out…fine." Abby dumped out the contents of the bowl and a cloud of flour rose into the air. She wrinkled her nose to subdue a sneeze.

"Uh-oh."

"What?"

"You're making bread, aren't you?"

Abby put her hands protectively over the mound of yeast dough, as if Jessica was looking over her shoulder. "Maybe."

"Maybe," Jessica repeated. "So that's a big yes. You know you only make bread when something is bothering you."

"That's not true." At least, not always. But Jessica was right. There was something very therapeutic about pummeling—*kneading*—bread dough.

"So, what's this new carpenter like? What's his name?"

"Are we playing Twenty Questions?" Abby asked. "Because I prefer I Spy. Or Scrabble."

"Hold on a sec, Abbs." Jessica didn't bother to muffle her voice. "I'll be right there, honey. I'm on the phone with Abby. She's making bread."

"Uh-oh." Tony's baritone boomed in the background.

"Okay, I'm back. Continue. New carpenter…"

"Quinn O'Halloran." Abby punched down the dough with a little more force than necessary.

"What's he like?"

Reserved came immediately to mind. Confident. *Incredibly good looking…*

Abby put the brakes on her thoughts, refusing to let them continue down that path. Too dangerous. "He works faster than Daniel, so the cabins might be ready for the grand opening."

"Then what's the problem…" Jessica's voice trailed off, replaced by an audible smack as her palm connected with her forehead. "I'm sorry. Stupid question. Sometimes I forget."

"Don't apologize," Abby said quietly. "I want you to forget."

She wanted to forget.

"Does he make you uncomfortable?"

"Daniel recommended him."

"That doesn't answer my question."

Abby hesitated. She knew what Jessica was really asking but wasn't sure how to answer. Did Quinn make her uncomfortable? Yes. But not in the way her friend assumed.

"I'll talk to Tony." Jessica drew her own conclusion from the silence. "We can take a few days off. Drive up for the weekend."

Abby was touched by the offer. "And if you looked in the rearview mirror, you'd see Alex's Viper right behind you. We can't let him think that I'm afraid and calling for reinforcements."

"You're right," Jessica muttered. "He'd dispatch the deprogrammers and you'd be back in Illinois before sunset."

Somehow, her friend always managed to make Abby smile. "You should get back to Tony. He must be feeling neglected."

"It makes him appreciate me more."

The distinctly masculine snort that followed the comment made them both giggle.

"I'm praying for you," Jessica whispered.

"I know. I wouldn't be here if you weren't."

"You give me way too much credit. You're there because you listened to God and faced your fears."

Listened to God, Abby hoped so. Faced her fears? That was more difficult. Especially when they kept popping up like targets in a shooting gallery.

"One step at a time, remember?" Jessica said, as if she'd read Abby's mind. "And if this O'Halloran guy makes you nervous, you can find someone to take his place. It's okay."

"He doesn't make me nervous. Not like that." Abby had worked hard to overcome her wariness of strangers but there were times it crept back in, especially if she was in a confined space with someone she didn't know. Or if someone turned up when she wasn't expecting them.

With Quinn, it had been both.

The strange thing was, Abby had felt as if he'd somehow sensed her unease. There were times she could have sworn that he'd stepped away from her on purpose. Given her some space. And the few times they had been in close proximity, instead of feeling vulnerable, Abby had felt…safe.

She hadn't experienced that before.

That was what made her nervous.

Quinn flipped over on his back and swam leisurely to shore, letting the cool water flow over the kinks in his muscles. He'd replaced the last window in the cabin as the sun began to sink into the horizon, making the trees look as if they'd been planted in liquid gold. Venus, the first planet to appear in the evening sky, winked at him through a tear in the bank of apricot clouds above his head.

After working in the hot sun all afternoon, Quinn had looked forward to cooling off in the lake with a relaxing swim. The cooling off part was successful. The relaxing part, not so much. His thoughts weren't cooperating.

Not with Abby Porter all tangled up in them.

Two weeks. That's all I can spare.

The words he'd said to Alex came back to mock him. Because less than eight hours later, he was ready to bolt. Faye would understand about the air conditioner….

Who was he kidding? If that was the only thing at stake, he would be on his way back to town by now.

Reaching the dock, Quinn grabbed on to the ladder and pulled himself up. By the time he toweled off and started back to the cabin, the low drone in the bushes made him glad he'd repaired the hole in the screened porch.

There was no sign of Lady. She'd wanted to swim out to the raft with him but Quinn had made her stay behind. Because what the little dog lacked in size, she more than made up for in volume. If a car pulled into the driveway, Lady let him know about it. No one could get past her without sounding the alarm. Because she rivaled the best system O'Halloran Security had to offer, Quinn was willing to turn over guard duty to her for a while.

He'd never worked as a bodyguard with the intent of staying as far away as possible from the client before, but Quinn was up to the challenge this time.

Whenever his traitorous thoughts had started to conjure up Abby Porter's smile or her laugh, all Quinn had to do was squelch them by recalling the phone conversation he'd overheard through the cabin window. A glimpse into the woman's true nature. She was like so many of the people who'd hired him when he was with Hamlin. Sweet and personable as long as everything went their way. Ready to use the weight of their name and bank account number when it didn't. Like Serena Raynes.

Quinn's stomach rumbled suddenly, chiding him for turning down Abby's offer to cook for him. He ignored it. There was nothing wrong with a good old-fashioned can of sodium-saturated broth with pieces of mystery meat floating in it.

He stopped short as he entered the kitchen. And then looked around to make sure he hadn't walked into the wrong cabin by mistake. Nope. The canvas duffel bag containing his clothes was on the floor where he'd left it; flannel shirt tossed over the back of the sofa.

Quinn turned back to the old trestle table. It was covered with a crisp, white tablecloth that hadn't been there when he'd left the cabin to go for a swim. Someone—and he had a pretty good idea who that someone was—had also taken the time to artfully arrange a place setting that rivaled the ones he'd seen in four-star restaurants. China plate. More silverware than Quinn knew what to do with. A crystal decanter filled with ice water.

The centerpiece was a covered casserole dish. Which

Quinn eyed as if it were a ticking package that had been delivered in the mail.

Cautiously, he lifted the lid. And choked on a laugh.

Macaroni and cheese. At least Quinn figured that's what it was. It didn't look quite the same as what he was used to.

"Lady!" Quinn bellowed.

She appeared in the doorway, stubby tail wagging. A dog biscuit roughly the size of Quinn's tennis shoe clamped between her teeth. Still, Lady managed to make a noise that sounded more like a quack than a bark.

"Your timing is a little off." Quinn rolled his eyes. "You're supposed to make a ruckus before someone breaks in, not after."

Not in the least concerned by the reprimand, Lady turned and trotted off to finish her supper.

Quinn decided it would be foolish of him not to do the same.

It didn't mean he'd changed his opinion of Abby Porter.

Abby's alarm clock—the dozen crows that perched in the pine tree outside her bedroom window every morning—went off at quarter to five.

Right on schedule.

Ordinarily, she loved to wake up to the sound. As soon as the sky began to lighten, they met in the branches and held what would probably be considered a lively coffee clutch in the aviary world. Minus the coffee. The noise level reminded her a little of the people who crowded into the booths at the Grapevine Café to exchange news. Abby relied on the birds to wake her up every morning but in this instance, morning had come way too soon.

Rolling over, Abby fought the temptation to pull the quilt over her head and close her eyes for a few more minutes. She could blame the total absence of sleep on the gigantic bowl of Moose Tracks ice cream she'd eaten at midnight…or on Quinn O'Halloran.

The ice cream was the obvious choice. Quinn the more honest one.

Abby shifted restlessly as she recalled the abrupt change in his attitude after she'd excused herself to speak to Derek Carlson's landlord.

A month before she'd left Chicago, Tony and Jessica had introduced her to Derek, a young man who had recently joined their congregation and was trying to turn his life around after serving time in jail for theft.

Abby had not only arranged for the hotel to hire Derek as a line cook but she'd found an apartment for him in a building near the hotel so he could ride his bicycle to work. Unfortunately, when Derek's record came to light, the landlord had changed his mind about renting to him.

Derek had left a message on her phone, telling her the landlord had added an amendment to the contract. He wanted a year's lease, backed up by a two-month security deposit, or he wouldn't let Derek take the apartment.

The landlord's latest obstacle forced Abby to perform her best imitation of Alex at his most autocratic, hoping she could pull it off. But when she ended the conversation and had gone outside to find Quinn, he barely spared a glance in her direction.

On her way back to the lodge, it occurred to Abby that he might have taken offense at her less than enthusiastic response to what he considered edible food.

Abby groaned and buried her face in the pillow, once again scolding herself for her lack of sensitivity.

Quinn had come right out and said he wanted to work as many hours as possible because he needed the additional income. If a man was forced to be frugal with his finances, then canned soup was not only easy but it didn't strain the budget, either.

Abby believed that actions spoke louder than words but she had her own little twist on the saying.

The best kind of apology was served warm from the oven.

Hence the double batch of gooey, homemade macaroni and cheese.

There'd been no sign of Quinn when she'd knocked on the door of the cabin, so she'd bribed her way past Lady with a jumbo, whole-wheat dog biscuit.

A single bare lightbulb flickering in the kitchen ceiling was the only thing holding the evening shadows at bay. The room looked so stark and unappealing that Abby hadn't been able to resist the urge to spruce things up a bit. She'd set the table, left the casserole dish where Quinn couldn't miss it and then spent a restless night wondering how he felt about the peace offering she'd left.

"You're *still* thinking about it," Abby muttered.

Mulligan's impatient woof at the bottom of the stairs reminded her that the grace period for delivering his breakfast kibbles had officially expired.

"Five more minutes," Abby called, reaching for the Bible on her nightstand.

After moving into her new home, Abby had taken Jessica's advice and started reading through the Psalms. Her friend must have known she'd find encouragement in the verses that reminded her not to be afraid. To trust God.

And there were a lot of them. She would pick one out and think about it while taking Mulligan for his morning walk around the lake.

The peaceful lap of the water against the shoreline and the whisper of wind in the trees provided the perfect start to the day. Time to memorize one of her "walking verses." As much as there was to accomplish, Abby didn't want to get so focused on fixing up the lodge that she neglected to seek out the One who'd led her there in the first place.

As she got dressed, she heard the staccato tap of a hammer outside the window. For some reason, it didn't surprise her that Quinn was an early riser, too. She resisted the urge to look out the window and went downstairs to the kitchen.

She filled a thermos with coffee and grabbed one of the biscuits she'd made. When she opened the door, two dogs stood there, looking up at her with hopeful expressions.

Abby smiled.

"The more the merrier, I suppose. Let's go."

Chapter Five

"**W**here is my sister?"

"Porter." Quinn removed the nail pinched in the corner of his lips. He wouldn't have answered his cell except for the fact he'd decided to allow Abby's brother one phone call a day. He'd also decided to get it over with as soon as possible. "What's wrong? Your satellite imagery isn't working this morning?"

"Funny," Alex growled. "Now answer the question."

"Is this a test?"

"Yes."

Quinn eyed the board, held the nail in place and gave it a solid whack with the hammer. "I haven't seen her yet, so my guess is that she's still sleeping."

"Your guess." Alex repeated the words. "It's your job to *know.* It's seven-thirty and Abby's routine is to be awake and going by five."

"I've been here twenty-four hours," Quinn pointed out mildly. "Not quite enough time to get to know her routine." Other than forcing her way into his kitchen and offering her opinion about grocery lists. Breaking and entering, armed with macaroni and cheese… Quinn stuck another nail between his lips to circumvent a smile.

"She goes for a walk around the lake every morning."

"If you're six hours away and you know that, what do you need me for?"

"The only reason I know is because Abby *told* me she does. A prayer walk, whatever that is." Alex's tone made it clear he didn't much care. "And you should be with her."

"Abby is fine." Quinn might not be sure where Abby was at the moment, but he was convinced of that much. "And you're spending an awful lot of money for no reason."

"I have a reason." Alex's voice tightened. "It's called peace of mind."

Quinn's gaze drifted to the curve of the shoreline, where the trees formed a living wall that blocked out the sunlight. "If it makes you feel better, I'll check on her."

"I'd appreciate it." Sarcasm leaked into Alex's voice. "Why do I get the feeling that you aren't taking this seriously, O'Halloran."

"You're taking it seriously enough for both of us. If you aren't happy, maybe you should find someone else." *Sorry, Faye,* Quinn thought. *I'll get you a bigger fan.*

"You agreed to keep an eye on Abby. You can't do that unless you're *with* her."

Quinn didn't appreciate the reminder. Because it was true.

"Is your private investigator having any luck?"

"He's narrowed it down to three possibilities."

"No kidding? Only three?"

Alex laughed. "O'Halloran…"

"I'm fired?" Quinn interrupted hopefully.

"You're quite the comedian."

"But still employed?"

"Yes."

Quinn was afraid Porter was going to say that. What he didn't understand was why. So he asked.

"I told you. I wanted the best."

"You didn't ask Ken Raynes for a reference, did you?" Quinn dropped the question like a gauntlet.

Alex didn't pick it up. "I hired the right person."

Quinn wished he felt the same way.

"'The name of the Lord is a strong tower. The righteous runs into it and is safe.'"

Abby said the words out loud, letting them soak into her soul.

For too long, she'd taken refuge in the Porter name. Hidden behind the wealth and privilege—and protection—it afforded. Although both she and Alex worked hard to ensure the success of the business their parents had started, Abby knew their inheritance gave them access to resources most people didn't have.

It was the reason she'd been determined to do things on her own when she purchased the property on Mirror Lake. And why she hadn't told anyone in town about her connection to Porter Hotels.

Alex thought she'd lost her mind, but Abby knew that something different had happened. She'd found *peace* of mind.

She wasn't going to trust the Porter name to keep her safe anymore. Or to define who she was. There were other names she put her hope in now.

Savior. Deliverer. Prince of Peace. Shield. Fortress.

Reading through the Psalms and discovering the names of God was like panning for gold. The verses helped her sift out her old way of thinking—the doubts and fears and insecurities—until the truth remained.

It felt like an adventure. One she wouldn't have had the

courage to embark on without finding strength in God's promises.

Her thoughts drifted back to Quinn. Something that had been happening on a frequent—and rather disturbing—basis over the past twenty-four hours.

Was he a believer?

Quinn seemed so...guarded. And a flicker of doubt had appeared in his eyes when she'd told him that Alex thought he had a better plan for her life than God did.

Jessica's husband had mentioned that some men had a difficult time surrendering their lives to God because it was hard to relinquish control. Abby had discovered the irony in that when she'd examined her own heart. She *didn't* have control. Accepting that hadn't been scary, it had set her free.

She'd been praying for months that Alex would discover that same truth....

And Quinn, Lord. If he doesn't know You.

Rounding a corner, Abby stepped off the worn path that meandered along the shoreline to follow the one she'd discovered a few weeks ago. Mulligan, who knew their destination, played tag with Lady through the underbrush.

As the trees opened into a clearing, Abby's heart lifted at the sight of the chapel. It hadn't been listed in the property description, so when Abby had stumbled upon it one day while chasing after Mulligan, who'd been chasing after a rabbit, it felt as if she'd been given a gift. The tiny, fieldstone building was empty except for six wooden pews arranged in front of a cross fashioned from rough-hewn timbers.

Along with the kitchen, it had become one of her favorite retreats.

"Sorry, you two. No dogs allowed."

Mulligan and Lady, who'd been waiting for her to catch

up, seemed to understand because they flopped down in the grass a few feet away from the weathered door.

Abby left the door open a few inches to let some fresh air circulate inside the building as she slipped past them.

The scent of lemon oil lingered in the air. She'd polished the pews until she could see her reflection, but other than that she'd left the chapel the way she'd found it. Even though it would benefit from some simple repairs, Abby was reluctant to change a thing. At first she wasn't sure she wanted to let the guests know about it, but decided it would be selfish to keep it a secret.

She slid into the first pew and closed her eyes, trying to remember her walking verse.

The name of the Lord is a strong tower...

A hand clamped down on her shoulder and Abby surged to her feet, her instincts fueled by the adrenaline coursing through her veins.

In the time it took Abby to draw her next breath, she had flipped the person onto his back, neutralizing the threat.

Quinn.

Quinn lay flat on his back, staring up at the beamed ceiling.

A blurry image of Abby's face appeared above him, the silver-green eyes wide. He blinked. Because incredibly enough, it looked as if she were...

"Smiling," Quinn groaned. "Why are you smiling?"

"Because it worked." Abby dropped to her knees beside him.

He tried to lift his head but little white spots danced in front of his eyes. Suddenly there were two Abbys. And *both* of them were smiling. "What worked?"

"The takedown. It's a self-defense move—"

"I know what it is." Quinn pushed his fingertips against the floor to get some leverage so he could sit up. And chase the spots away. "But why did you practice it on me?"

Abby looked a little uncertain now. "You...surprised me."

"I surprised *you?*"

When he looked through the opening in the door and saw Abby sitting in the pew, he'd thought she was crying. Her head was bent, chin against her chest. Shoulders slumped. It had propelled him to her side in an instant.

The next thing he knew, he was flat on his back, staring up at the ceiling.

"Are you all right?"

"Too late," Quinn muttered. "I think those are the first words I should have heard. Not 'it worked.'"

"I'm sorry." Abby tried unsuccessfully to subdue her excitement. "It's just that I studied that move in a book and I wasn't sure it would really work."

"Glad I could help... *Ouch.*" Quinn pushed himself into a sitting position and lifted a hand to explore the lump he was sure had to be sprouting from the back of his head. But Abby's hands got there first, tunneling through his hair. Exploring his scalp.

Making him see spots all over again.

Quinn swallowed hard. "Next time just knock me unconscious."

"What?"

"Never mind." Time for a countermove. He inched away.

Abby scooted closer. "No blood. I don't think there's any swelling, either."

Quinn gaped at her. She actually sounded a little disappointed. "Just a mild concussion, huh? I guess I'm lucky this concrete floor has some give to it."

"It's pine, not concrete." Abby leaned in until they were almost nose to nose. Close enough for Quinn to see an intriguing emerald fleck in one of her silver-green eyes. Breathe in the fresh scent of her shampoo—along with that intriguing hint of cinnamon. "Your pupils aren't dilated."

The side effects from being so close to Abby were proving to be greater than any caused by a bump on the head.

Ignoring the pain that streaked up the back of his neck, Quinn lurched to his feet. "Thank you, Dr. Porter. Did you read a book on how to diagnose the damage you caused after you read a book on how to cause the damage?"

"Okay, maybe you do have a concussion." Abby reached for him and Quinn drew back. "I won't flip you again. Promise." The engaging smile she flashed in his direction was more dangerous than her amateur ninja skills.

Now that the spots had begun to fade—and Abby no longer had her hands in his hair—his thoughts began to clear. "I'm not sure why you *flipped me* in the first place."

"I told you. You surprised me." Abby bit her lip and turned away. "How did you find me up here? Did you need something?"

An explanation, that's what he needed.

Quinn stared at her; the instincts he no longer trusted kicked into red alert. Most people, even if startled, would have reacted differently. An involuntary jerk. A gasp. Abby, on the other hand, had felt his hand on her shoulder and treated him as a…threat.

Why?

"A how-to book on self-defense," he ventured casually. "Is that what you consider light reading?"

"Oh, you know…" Abby's gaze slid away from him. "Because you never know."

As far as explanations went, it meant nothing. And everything.

Quinn rubbed the back of his head, wondering if he should push the issue.

Abby noticed the gesture and had the good sense to at least *pretend* she felt guilty about tossing him onto a hardwood floor. "Does it still hurt?"

"Only my pride."

Abby smiled again. "If that's all, then *Dr. Porter* guarantees you'll make a full recovery."

Quinn wasn't so sure. The damage to his head was minimal. At the moment he was more concerned about the potential damage to his heart.

Chapter Six

$\mathbf{A}$bby spent the remainder of the morning staining trim in the library and berating herself for her response when Quinn had shown up at the chapel and touched her shoulder.

She wouldn't have blamed him if *his* response had been to quit on the spot.

If Quinn questioned her sanity for converting a dilapidated former Bible camp into a bed-and-breakfast—and there was evidence to support that theory—then what did he think of her now?

All he'd done was put his hand on her shoulder to get her attention and she had sent him sprawling.

And then, to make matters worse, she'd smiled.

Smiled.

And touched him, an inner voice reminded her, adding another item to her list of crimes.

Checked for bruises, Abby corrected, even as a memory pushed its way in. The silky slide of Quinn's hair between her fingers. The warmth of his skin. The way his eyes had darkened to charcoal—okay, possibly due to pain—when she'd knelt down next to him to see if he was showing signs of a concussion.

Stain dripped off the end of the foam brush and landed on her shoe instead of the drop cloth.

That did it.

A change of scenery was in order. Something to keep her mind off Quinn O'Halloran. Maybe it was time to devote some attention to the list of errands she'd been putting off for the last few days.

Abby poked her head out the door and called for Mulligan, jingling her car keys as an added incentive. He loved to sit in the passenger seat and stick his head out the window, lips turned inside out in a grin, while his ears flapped in the breeze like miniature wind socks.

After waiting another sixty seconds, it was clear that her faithful companion had abandoned her for the adorable cocker spaniel that had moved in next door.

Abby paused on her way to the garage, wondering whether she should walk down to the cabin and let Quinn know she would be gone for a few hours.

Since she'd barely seen him after they'd parted company that morning, she decided against it. He wouldn't even notice she was gone.

Coward.

True. But in this situation, Abby decided she could live with that. Her formal apology was cooling on the kitchen counter, so although she knew she had to face Quinn sooner or later, Abby picked later. She couldn't face him at the moment.

"Going somewhere?"

Abby froze. And turned toward the familiar voice. Quinn stood several yards away. Looking better than anyone had a right to in a plain white T-shirt and faded jeans. His hands were raised above his head as if he were surrendering.

A bubble of laughter escaped before she could prevent it. "Not funny."

"Who said I was joking? Never let it be said that Quinn O'Halloran doesn't learn from his mistakes." Something moved through Quinn's eyes like sunlight skimming the surface of the water. On anyone else, Abby would have recognized it as amusement. On Quinn…

No, it couldn't be. He couldn't actually be *teasing* her.

While she was trying to wrap her mind around that, his lips hitched up at the corners.

Abby's heart did a free fall to her toes.

It wasn't the polished, make-sure-you-get-my-best-side kind that she was used to having bestowed upon her. Not even close. And as far as smiles went, it probably wouldn't even register on a smile scale. If there was a smile scale. But none of that mattered because even the *hint* of a smile on Quinn O'Halloran's face packed enough punch to steal the breath from a woman's lungs.

While Abby struggled to draw a breath, the pointed look Quinn aimed at the keys dangling from her fingers reminded her that he'd asked a question.

"I have some errands to run in town."

"Mind if I tag along?"

It was the last thing she expected Quinn to say. And the last thing she wanted him to do. After all, the whole point of putting some distance between them was so she wouldn't think about Quinn for a few hours. It defeated the whole purpose if she actually brought him with her.

"I need a few things from the hardware store if I want to start the roof this afternoon," he added. "I was going to drive in later, but when I saw you walking to your car…"

He knew it would be silly to take separate vehicles to the same place. Abby knew it, too. That's why she gave in.

"I suppose."

Some of her reluctance must have crept into her voice because Quinn's eyebrow lifted. "Can you give me five minutes to wash up and put Lady in the cabin?"

"I don't mind if you bring her along."

The elusive smile came and went again. "You'd have her on your lap. Lady doesn't like the backseat."

"Neither does Mulligan. If we take your truck, we can all fit in front."

"My truck?" Quinn's expression was as astonished as if she'd suggested they fly to Mirror Lake.

"What's wrong with your truck?"

"Nothing. Except it's probably not as comfortable as your vehicle." The pointed look Quinn aimed at her lipstick-red convertible severed the connection his unexpected smile had created between them.

Before Abby could explain that the car hadn't been her choice, but a gift from Alex on her twenty-first birthday, Quinn was already striding back to the cabin.

Five minutes later, the four of them were wedged together into the cab of Quinn's pickup. Lady curled sedately up in her lap while Mulligan sat in the middle, content to give up his usual window seat for the entertainment of watching the tree-shaped air freshener dance from Quinn's rearview mirror.

Abby pulled a piece of paper out of her bag and skimmed the contents. "Have you lived in Mirror Lake very long?"

Quinn didn't answer so Abby wasn't sure he'd heard her. She tried again. "Have you—"

"A while."

A while.

What did that mean? A month? A year? Ten years? The shuttered expression on Quinn's face made her curious.

"How much time will you need in town?" He neatly tried to change the subject. Which made Abby even more curious.

"Not more than two hours. A friend of mine recommended that I buy from local artists when it's time to put the finishing touches on the inn. Do you know anyone in the area I could talk to?"

"Artists? Not that I can think of." Quinn slanted a look at her over Mulligan's bushy head. "Stop in and ask at the Grapevine Café. I'm sure someone there would know."

"I love that place."

"Why?"

"It reminds me of the diners on those old TV shows. Vinyl booths. Plastic ferns in the window. An old-fashioned soda fountain. A jukebox. Everyone talks to everyone else. It's like stepping back in time."

Exactly why Quinn avoided it.

What he had a difficult time believing was that Kate Nichols's café appealed to Abby, whose last name opened doors to the best of the best. The Porter Hotels' in-house restaurants boasted four-star ratings and required a tie to get past the maître d'.

Abby might view the "everyone talks to everyone else" as a quaint, small-town feature but from Quinn's perspective, it was gossip, plain and simple.

The locals loved the café because a cup of coffee was cheaper than subscribing to the *Mirror Lake Register* and the news more timely. They also had the place to themselves, as the tourists who migrated north in the summer usually bypassed the Grapevine on their quest to find something a little more upscale.

It had also become a popular teenage hangout over the years, even before Kate's parents had turned the place over to her. Quinn had avoided it back then.

The same way he did now.

He shouldn't have suggested to Abby that she go there for the information she was seeking. Not that Quinn expected his name to come up, but it had before. Thanks to his father, the O'Halloran name had been the topic of conversation more times than Quinn wanted to remember.

"I have to talk to Mayor Dodd." Abby nibbled thoughtfully on the end of a pen. "Something about a community celebration that's coming up."

"Labor Day weekend. Reflection Days," Quinn muttered, barely avoiding another pothole as he tore his gaze away from the velvet-soft curve of her lower lip.

Laughter flowed through the cab of his truck. "Clever."

Quinn wasn't surprised Abby had made the connection so quickly, but a lot of people didn't get it. "I suppose that's one word for it."

"What would you call it?" She tilted her head and a wisp of hair drifted across her cheek. Quinn tightened his grip on the steering wheel so he wouldn't do something stupid. Like brush it away.

A two-day forced march down memory lane, that's what he would call it. But he couldn't tell Abby that. Not without opening a Pandora's box full of questions he didn't want to answer.

"An excuse for the Chamber of Commerce to increase their annual budget." There. That was safe. It also happened to be the truth.

Abby clucked her tongue. "Were you born this cynical?"

"You could say that." Quinn had been born an O'Halloran, so the two kind of went hand in hand.

"Well, I think you're blessed to live in a town like Mirror Lake. Even if it's only been for *a while*."

Quinn didn't miss the emphasis Abby put on the last words and a reluctant smile tugged at his lips. Her sense of humor and buoyant personality continued to surprise—and, if he were honest—charm him.

Except that Quinn didn't want to be charmed.

He kept his eyes focused on the road, hoping Abby would take his silence as an indication that he didn't want to talk.

She didn't.

"So what does Reflection Days involve? Other than padding the town budget?"

"Mirror Lake started out as a logging town in the 1800s. A lot of the families can trace their ancestry back to the original founders." Quinn found it more than a little ironic that he should be the one to explain the history of Reflection Days. "There's not much holding it together anymore. When businesses started to close and kids grew up and didn't come back, the city council got nervous. They decided to hold an annual community pride celebration to remind people of the values Mirror Lake was originally founded on."

"I think it's a wonderful idea."

"You might change your mind when Mayor Dodd tries to guilt you on to one of his committees. That's the thing about Reflection Days. All the local businesses are expected to participate."

Except for O'Halloran Security, of course.

When Quinn had moved back to Mirror Lake the summer before, no one had approached him about contributing in some way to the weekend-long celebration. If he'd had any doubt the community wasn't eager to throw out the welcome mat for another O'Halloran, there was his proof.

"Do you think so?" Instead of looking concerned, something Quinn would expect from a person who had enough work to keep her busy round the clock for the next year, Abby's eyes sparkled with anticipation.

Quinn had never been so relieved to see the Welcome to Mirror Lake sign up ahead. "I'll find a place to park the truck and meet you back there in a few hours. Don't worry about the dogs. Slim Peterson keeps his Irish setter at the hardware store so they'll have a chance to stretch their legs running up and down the paint aisle."

"Thanks. I'll try not to take too long." Abby slipped the list back into her purse. "I still have to finish staining trim when we get back... Quinn, look. There's a parking space."

Right in front of the Grapevine Café.

He cruised past it. "Sorry." Not a bit. "Missed it."

"Because you stepped on the gas instead of the brake," Abby said under her breath.

Quinn found another spot farther down the street. In front of Happy's Engine Repair and as far from the café's enormous plate-glass windows as possible.

If word hadn't already gotten out that he and Abby were working together, Quinn wasn't going to deliberately provide grist for the local rumor mill.

Abby pulled down the visor and frowned. "Where's the mirror?"

"Mirror?" Quinn echoed.

"The mirror that comes as a standard feature on every visor," Abby said. Slowly. Enunciating her words as if explaining something to a very small child.

"There is no mirror."

She sighed and shifted in her seat so she was facing him. "Well?"

"Well, what?"

"You're going to have to be my mirror. How is my face?" She stared straight ahead, schooling her features until she resembled one of the marble statues he'd seen in the Chicago Institute of Art.

Quinn eyed her suspiciously. "Is this a trick question?"

"Of course not." Abby's sigh stirred the wisps of sunstreaked hair on her forehead. She rephrased the question. "How do I *look?*"

Stunning was the first word that came to Quinn's mind before he could put it on lockdown. "Fine."

"You're sure?" Abby looked more anxious that a trip to the Grapevine Café warranted. "My hair isn't a mess? My lipstick hasn't worn off? No one knows me very well so I want to make a good impression."

"Your hair is…fine. Lipstick…" Quinn's breath hitched in his throat. To answer the lipstick question meant he had to look at her lips. Something he'd deliberately avoided for the entire ten-minute car ride into town. And had planned to deliberately avoid for the next two weeks. "Also fine."

"That wasn't so bad, now was it?" Abby grinned, tucked her purse under one arm and hugged her smelly old dog with the other.

She had no idea.

Quinn needed to do something to restore his equilibrium and since cynicism had always worked well for him in the past…

"But if you wanted to make a good impression, you should have driven your convertible into town."

Alone.

Abby wrinkled her nose. "Shame on you," she scolded lightly. "That sounds like something someone who judges a person by the kind of car they drive—or don't drive—would say."

She marched away, the heels of her cute little sandals clicking against the sidewalk.

Quinn stared after her in disbelief.

If he wasn't mistaken, Abby Porter had just accused him—Quinn O'Halloran—of being a snob.

Chapter Seven

❧

"What can I get for you, Abby?" Kate Nichols slid into the seat across from her with a welcoming smile.

Abby, who couldn't imagine her brother ever joining his guests at their table with such unaffected ease, smiled back. The owner of the Grapevine Café couldn't have been more than a few years older than she was, but the lively snap in Kate's shamrock-green eyes hinted she was up to any challenge that came her way.

Abby felt a pinch of envy.

We're working on it, aren't we, Lord?

"Just coffee." Abby's gaze drifted to the slices of pie rotating in a dessert carousel a few yards away from the booth.

Kate arched a copper brow. "Strawberry, peach or apple?"

"Strawberry."

"Strawberry it is." Kate leaned forward. "So what brings you into town? I haven't seen you since the service last Sunday morning."

Abby winced at the memory.

Exhausted from working well past midnight, Abby had

started to nod off during the video clip Pastor Wilde had played during the adult Sunday school hour. A discreet nudge from Kate's elbow had saved her from acute embarrassment.

Abby would have scooted away right after the class ended but Kate had caught up to her at the door, blocking her escape with an enormous leather study Bible. Something in the young woman's warm personality and mischievous smile had reminded her of Jessica, so she'd accepted Kate's invitation to sit with her during the worship service.

"I still can't believe I did that."

"Don't worry about it. I know what exhaustion feels like. I'm up by 4:00 a.m. making pies three times a week. Believe me, you'll have a chance to return the favor someday." The soft laugh that followed the promise put Abby instantly at ease.

"I will."

Kate turned toward a pack of adolescent boys jostling their way between the tables, their destination the jukebox in the corner. The movement set her cap of fiery red corkscrew curls bouncing.

"No music for five minutes. We're trying to have a conversation here," she barked out.

The boys froze in their tracks and did an immediate about-face, slinking back to the booth they'd occupied moments before.

"If I have to listen to 'Born to Be Wild' one more time, I'm pulling the plug on that relic," Kate muttered. "Missy! Read that book during your break. We need two cups of coffee and a piece of strawberry pie over here."

The willowy teenage girl behind the counter snapped to attention, blushing, and hurried to obey.

"My brother would love you," Abby said without thinking.

"What?" Kate's eyes widened.

"As an employee," Abby amended quickly. "Alex owns

a…restaurant." Or four. Restaurants which happened to be located in the hotels he also owned, but she saw no point in mentioning that. "He appreciates 'highly motivated people.'"

Unless it was his sister, of course. When it came to her, Alex appreciated it when Abby was highly motivated in a place where he could keep an eye on her.

Kate shrugged. "If you aren't highly motivated around here, you don't survive. Which is why you'll do just fine. It was sheer genius to buy that old camp and turn it into a bed-and-breakfast."

Abby hadn't expected the compliment but it bloomed inside her. "There's still a lot of work to do."

"When isn't there?" Kate aimed a wink at Missy, who'd sidled up with the pie and two cups of coffee. "Refill the boys' glasses and take ten, sweetheart. You're not going to be any good to me if you spend the whole afternoon wondering what's going to happen at the end of chapter three."

Missy's wide smile exposed twin rows of metal braces. "Thanks, Kate!" She darted away.

"Chapter three?"

"I facilitate a book club for high school girls. It meets here once a month during the summer," Kate explained. "They get homemade pizza and chocolate cake and I get a chance to reread the books I loved at that age. It's a win-win situation."

"It sounds like a lot of fun." Abby emptied the contents of a sugar packet into her coffee. "And I think it's great you take the time to organize something for them."

Kate waved her spoon in the air, as if brushing aside the compliment. "The kids' main complaint is that there isn't a lot to do around here. This is my way of encouraging them to 'bloom where they're planted,' so to speak. You don't know how many times I hear the girls say they can't wait to graduate and move away, never to return."

"Did you ever feel that way?"

"Call me crazy, but no. I never did. I happen to think Mirror Lake has a lot to offer—but I guess it depends on what you're looking for." Kate smiled. "You must know what I'm talking about. I mean, you moved here on purpose, you brave girl."

Brave? It was a word Abby never would have chosen to describe herself. Her faith had given her the courage to start a new life in Mirror Lake but there were times she still battled doubt.

"The book club is always open to new members," Kate continued. "If you're interested."

"It's tempting…" Abby hesitated, not wanting to be rude.

"But totally unrealistic," Kate finished. "I understand. You've got your hands full with that place. I suppose it's slow going without Daniel Redstone there."

Abby wasn't surprised Kate had heard about Daniel's windfall. As much the carpenter talked about fishing, he'd probably turned cartwheels down the middle of Main Street after he'd won the vacation.

"He sent over his partner yesterday, so I'm still on schedule for the grand opening."

"Partner?"

"Quinn O'Halloran."

"Quinn—" Kate, who'd taken a sip from her cup, suddenly began to cough.

"Are you all right?" Abby plucked a napkin out of the metal holder and pressed it into Kate's hand.

"I think so," she wheezed, dabbing the cloth against her streaming eyes.

"Do you know Quinn?" Abby asked, hoping the question didn't sound like shameless curiosity. It was merely…curiosity. Without the shameless.

"A little. He grew up here but we were a few years apart in high school." Kate's voice crackled and she tried to smooth it out with another sip of coffee. "He left town right after graduation. No one saw him for years and then he showed up after his dad died. I didn't realize he was working for you."

"Only until Daniel comes back," Abby said, still processing what Kate had just told her. If Quinn had grown up in Mirror Lake, why hadn't he mentioned that when she'd asked him how long he'd lived in the area?

"He's helped Daniel out in the past, I suppose," Kate murmured. "But Quinn isn't—"

"Kate," a plaintive voice interrupted. "Can we play a song now?" One of the boys she'd shooed away appeared beside the booth. "It's been more than five minutes."

"Sure. Streisand or the Beach Boys. Your pick."

Glowering, the teenager stomped back to the booth.

"It's important to give kids choices." The twinkle in Kate's green eyes belied her serious tone. "Now, what were we talking about?"

"Quinn." Abby leaned forward, more than ready to return to the previous topic of their discussion.

She wanted to know the reason behind Kate's strange reaction when Abby had mentioned that Quinn was filling in for Daniel. And what Kate had been about to say right before they'd been interrupted.

"Miss Porter!" The bells on the door accompanied Mayor Dodd's boisterous greeting. "I knew I'd find you here!"

"Not that a person has a whole lot of options in a town this size," Kate whispered as she picked up her cup and slid out of the booth. "I think this is the perfect time to check over the dinner menu."

A half hour later, Abby knew why her new friend had made a quick getaway. While Quinn had managed to condense the purpose behind Reflection Days in a few short sentences, Mayor Dodd expounded on it as if he were standing behind a pulpit on a Sunday morning.

Abby had been introduced to him briefly after she'd moved to Mirror Lake. As round as he was tall, the mayor bore a striking resemblance to a garden gnome. Blue eyes blazed beneath snow-white eyebrows that merged together like an unclipped hedge over the bridge of his nose. Sideburns connected a flowing salt-and-pepper beard to the thick mustache that obscured his upper and lower lip. What it didn't obscure was the toothpick that jutted out of the corner of his mouth and kept time with every word he spoke.

"...the Chamber of Commerce welcomes new businesses to the area. You give to the community, you get back." Mayor Dodd's coffee cup came down between them like a gavel to emphasize the point.

"I'd be happy to—"

"Good. Good." The toothpick bobbed in approval. "We're one judge short for the Reflection Day parade."

Behind the counter, Abby saw Kate make a slashing gesture against her throat. "Um—"

"Good. Good. I'll have my wife call you with the details. She's in charge of the parade committee."

Abby decided that Kate must have been directing the gesture toward the boys crowded around the jukebox. Judging a parade didn't sound like a huge responsibility. And she was looking forward to getting involved in the community.

Abby happened to glance at the clock and gasped. "I'm sorry, Mayor Dodd. I have to go."

The toothpick drooped like a cat's tail on a rainy day. "But we haven't talked about your nomination for the Main Street beautification project yet—"

"Mayor?" Kate breezed up to the booth. "I've got one slice of apple pie left. On the house, if you're interested."

The blue eyes brightened. "On the house? Good. Good."

Abby sent the café owner a grateful look as she snatched up her purse. "How much do I owe you for the coffee?"

"Forget about it." Kate lowered her voice. "You earned it. FYI, the mayor's won the pie eating contest five years in a row. Six slices in three minutes and twelve seconds. Now go."

As Abby made a break for it, the opening beat of "Born to Be Wild" followed her out the door. Stepping into the warm afternoon sunshine, she scanned both sides of the street but there was no sign of Quinn. Or the truck.

Great. He'd kidnapped her dog and left her stranded in Mirror Lake.

"It's about time."

Quinn caught the wadded-up piece of paper that came sailing toward him as he walked into the office.

"That bad, huh?"

"Let me count the ways." Faye crossed her arms. "Your part-time guys are struggling for dominance. If this was *Survivor,* I'd vote them both off the island. Mel Burdock calls every few hours, complaining his house isn't getting the *un-divided attention* you promised when he hired you…and it's five hundred degrees in here today because my stubborn boss won't swallow his pride and let me buy an air conditioner for the office."

"Don't exaggerate. It can't be more than a hundred and fifty." Quinn raked a hand through his hair. "But go on."

"Thank you. I will." Faye picked up an envelope and waved

it at him. "This letter from Jeff Gaines came in the mail and every time I get tempted to steam it open, I eat a piece of candy instead. I've gained three pounds in the last two hours."

Quinn held out his hand.

"Candy or the letter?"

"Both."

Faye complied. "Now be a good boy and stand still while I read it over your shoulder."

"What would I do without you and your total disregard for the fact that I'm the one who signs your paycheck?"

"Is that what you call it?" she asked tartly. "To my way of thinking, a paycheck should cover more than a cup of coffee at the Grapevine."

"Kate's coffee *is* expensive." Quinn grinned, used to Faye's acerbic sense of humor. "I'll be back in a few minutes."

She reached up and patted his cheek. "I hope it's good news, honey."

He did, too. But it took two laps around the office before Quinn opened the envelope. If his bid was accepted, he could tell Alex Porter he wouldn't have time to work at the lodge, looking for threats that didn't exist…and be forced to deal with the unexpected feelings Abby stirred inside of him.

She continued to astonish him. Her response to his comment about the car had left him reeling. To Quinn's knowledge, no one had ever accused *him,* even teasingly, of being a snob before.

No one had ever dropped him on the back of his head with a basic move from chapter one of an amateur's guide to self-defense book, either.

Or cut through his defenses with a single smile.

The sooner he was done with this assignment—and, he reminded himself, Abby Porter *was* an assignment—the better. Alex had hinted that she had moved to Mirror Lake on a whim; once she realized that the grim reality outweighed her dreams, she would return to Chicago.

Quinn didn't doubt it for a second. And he had no intention of letting Abby take a piece of his heart when she jumped into that little red convertible and drove away.

He took a deep breath and opened the envelope. Inside was an official letter from Gaines Developers. With Jeff Gaines's official signature at the bottom. Officially telling him that the deadline for the bid on the White Wolf Run condos had been adjusted due to extenuating circumstances.

Extenuating circumstances otherwise known as Alex Porter.

Quinn closed his eyes briefly.

Should he admire the guy's tenacity or withdraw the bid and walk away with his pride still intact? Quinn hadn't been guaranteed that O'Halloran Security would win the contract, but if Porter put in a good word for him with Jeff Gaines, it would level the playing field a little. Give the business a fighting chance.

Quinn wished he didn't need one.

But Mike O'Halloran had dragged the family name through the mud and every time Quinn took a step forward, it felt as if everyone's eyes were on him—watching to see if he left footprints.

The bells over the front door jingled, announcing the arrival of someone Quinn hoped was a potential customer. If it wasn't, he had no doubt that Faye would convince the person that O'Halloran Security had something they needed.

He wasn't sure what he'd do without her.

Quinn hadn't forgotten the day she'd shown up because it was the day he'd almost given up.

He'd only been in Mirror Lake a week but was already overwhelmed by the monumental task of repairing all the things that had suffered due to his father's neglect. The house. The business. A needy cocker spaniel. A stunted, dried-up rhododendron bush planted next to the front door of the office that looked to be in the same shape as everything else he'd inherited.

While Quinn had been kneeling in front of the rhododendron, examining it for signs of life, someone's finger had tapped his shoulder with the force of a woodpecker searching for its next meal.

It had been years since he'd seen her, but Quinn recognized Faye McAllister immediately. She was one of the people he'd told Abby about, a member of a family who could trace their origins to the founders of Mirror Lake. She'd driven a Cadillac almost as long as Main Street and made a full-time career out of being a doctor's wife.

Everyone in Mirror Lake respected Faye—although Quinn suspected there was a thin line between respect and terror. If she was a little brash and outspoken, people were willing to overlook it because Doc McAllister was just the opposite. A quiet, even-tempered man who made house calls.

Shortly after his return to Mirror Lake, Quinn had heard that Doc had passed away the previous fall, but he hadn't seen Faye around.

Until she'd found him.

"You don't answer the phone or the door," she snapped. "Shouldn't you be helping your paying customers?"

Quinn wanted to say that he would, if he had paying customers to help. Instead he'd asked, "Can I do something for you, Mrs. McAllister?"

"I don't know." Faye had glowered at him. "I locked my keys in my car. Is this place open for business or not?"

He'd almost said no.

"Yes."

"Then why is there a closed sign in the window? Why isn't someone in the office answering the phone?"

"Because I haven't hired someone to answer the phone yet." Quinn's frustration had reached its limit and spilled over into the next question. "When can you start?"

He'd waited, expecting Faye to club him over the head with her purse. To his astonishment, a smile had spread across her face.

"Tomorrow morning."

She'd arrived at eight o'clock the next day, a brown bag lunch in one hand and an African violet in the other, and took over the front office with the efficiency of a four-star general.

Faye had no computer skills and knew nothing about office management. Quinn kept her on anyway. Because his first two honest-to-goodness paying clients played bridge with her on Tuesday nights.

A coincidence? He didn't think so.

Staring down at the letter in his hand, Quinn tried to figure out the best way to explain the delay to Faye. One that would convince her not to call Jeff Gaines and demand an explanation of the "extenuating circumstances" herself.

On cue, the desk phone chirped at him.

"Yeah?"

"What's taking you so long?" Faye demanded. "Is the letter written in Chinese?"

He laughed. "No, it's in English."

"Then get out here and tell…wait a second. Someone is walking up the sidewalk."

She sounded disappointed. Quinn, on the other hand, was relieved. He'd slip out while Faye was occupied with the customer. Abby had asked for two hours and it was close to that now….

As he took a step toward the door, a familiar voice made Quinn's heart slam-dunk against his rib cage.

Abby.

She'd found him.

Chapter Eight

She'd gone to the wrong address.

Which meant Abby had five minutes to find the right one before it was time to meet up with Quinn again.

Plunging one hand into her purse, she tried to locate her list as an elderly woman, whose hair matched the sleeveless red blouse she wore, zipped toward her with an energy that was impressive, given the fact the building felt like a sauna.

"Can I help you?"

I doubt it.

Abby bit back the words before she said them out loud.

The address scrawled on the piece of paper had led her to a cement block eyesore two blocks off Main Street.

The sparsely furnished reception area, with its water-stained ceiling and dark paneled walls, gave Abby no clue as to what kind of business went on there but it couldn't have been the one she was looking for.

She mustered a friendly smile, an attempt to offset the grim work environment the poor woman had to deal with. "I hope so. I must have written down the wrong address."

"Maybe, maybe not. What are you looking for?"

"Fourteen Maplewood. There's supposed to be a locksmith there."

"Then you're in the right place."

"Really?" Abby caught herself. "That's…great." The floor sank beneath her foot as she took a step forward.

"Faye McAllister. Office manager." The woman extended a hand. "And you're in luck because the boss is in this afternoon. I'll let him know you're here."

"Oh." Now Abby was down to three minutes and counting. "I thought I'd make an appointment. I don't have a lot of time."

"That's all right. Neither does he." Faye McAllister tossed the cryptic words over her shoulder as she marched toward a crescent-shaped desk wedged between the counter and the wall.

Abby gnawed on her lower lip. Maybe she should call Quinn and let him know she'd be a few minutes late. As she searched in vain for her cell phone, which proved to be as elusive as her list, she heard the soft tread of footsteps coming toward her.

Abby looked up, the smile dying on her lips when she saw Quinn standing there.

Guilt zapped her conscience. She'd taken so long he'd been forced to track her down.

"I'm sorry, Quinn. I was just about to call you." Too bad she couldn't offer her phone as proof. "I need to hire a locksmith to key the rooms in the lodge but it shouldn't take long. I can meet you outside in a few minutes."

"Abby—"

"Abby?" Faye McAllister jumped into the silence and her eyes narrowed. "Abby *Porter?*"

"Y-yes." Abby's heart pitched. Was it possible the woman had recognized her name? She hadn't deliberately tried to keep it a secret, but she hadn't gone out of her way to tell people about her connection to Porter Hotels. She liked having people treat her the same way they would anyone else.

"And you need a locksmith."

"Y-yes."

"This is *O'Halloran* Security," Faye said.

"O'Halloran…" Heat that Abby couldn't blame on the sweltering air branded her cheeks.

There wasn't a sign in the yard. No logo on the door. Not even a number on the mailbox. As a newcomer to the area, how was she supposed to know who owned what?

Her gaze slid to Quinn. "One of your relatives is a lock-smith?"

Absolute silence followed the question.

"She doesn't know?" Faye aimed an accusing look at Quinn.

Abby looked from one to the other. "Know what?"

"You didn't *tell* her?"

"Tell me what?"

Quinn finally looked at her, the expression on his face similar to the one she'd seen earlier that morning. When he'd been lying on his back in the chapel.

"I'm the O'Halloran in O'Halloran Security."

Quinn saw the confusion darken Abby's eyes. "I don't understand."

"Get in line," Faye grumbled.

"Come back to my office so we can talk." Hopefully he'd come up with an explanation on the way there. But the first order of business was to separate Abby from the thoughtful gleam in his secretary's eyes.

"Office?" Abby repeated the word. "You have an *office?*"

"This way." With a stern look at Faye—who looked ready to follow—Quinn ushered Abby down the dim hallway.

He'd considered his office fairly passable but as they stepped inside, Quinn tried to see it through Abby's eyes.

Plaster and a fresh coat of paint didn't completely conceal the outline of fist-sized holes in the walls, evidence of Mike O'Halloran's frustration when things didn't go his way.

The oak desk was scarred but solid—and no one but Quinn would ever know that his initial sweep had revealed a cache of empty vodka bottles in the drawers.

The curtains Faye had strung up—without his permission, of course—not only provided color but concealed the hairline cracks in the glass that fanned out like a spider web along the top of the window casing.

Quinn had done what he could to make the office more customer-friendly, but replacing the business's outdated technology had been more of a priority than replacing the carpeting. Or the furniture....

"Abby, wait. Don't sit—" Down.

Before Quinn could finish the sentence, Abby had dropped into the captain's chair opposite his desk. When it immediately began to tilt like a faulty amusement park ride, she anchored one sandaled foot against the floor and looked up at him, waiting for an explanation.

Because Quinn was still working on that, he tried to stall.

"You didn't mention that you needed a locksmith."

"Maybe if you would have mentioned you *were* a locksmith, I would have mentioned that I needed one."

He couldn't argue with that logic.

"I can't believe—" Abby shook her head and Quinn sucked in a breath, waiting for the barrage of questions he knew would follow "—how amazing God is."

He blinked. "How what?"

"Amazing God is." Abby grinned. "I shouldn't be, should

I? Amazing is just part of who He is… It shouldn't surprise me when things like this happen. I mean, think about this."

Quinn had been. And all those thoughts centered on how to convince Abby that there was a valid reason why he was moonlighting as a carpenter.

She opened her arms and kicked off with her foot, sending the chair spinning in a wobbly circle.

Quinn would have leaped forward to stop her if he hadn't been so mesmerized by the sight. And the sound of her laughter.

"Every time I start to have doubts that I'm doing the right thing, He shows me that I'm on the right path." Abby planted both feet and stopped the chair midspin. "You don't know what I'm talking about, do you?"

"Not a clue."

"You. A locksmith. I can't believe it. You're already working on-site and you're familiar with the lodge and the cabins." Abby shook her head in wonder. "I don't have to meet with someone new and go over what needs to be done. You're there all day anyway. You can take some time to put new locks in, can't you?"

The chair had stopped spinning but Quinn still felt dizzy. Lack of oxygen prevented a person from thinking clearly, didn't it?

"Sure." The word almost got stuck in his throat. He'd expected Abby to be suspicious as to why he'd left his business to help get hers off the ground. But she was looking at him as if…

"You, Quinn O'Halloran, are an answer to prayer."

Quinn stared at her in disbelief. He wasn't an answer to prayer. In fact, he wasn't sure a man whose future at the moment was one big question mark could be an answer to anything.

He rejected the claim with a shake of his head. "I'm just the hired help."

Alex Porter's hired help.

"That's not true." Abby said it with so much sincerity that for a moment, Quinn was actually tempted to believe her. But what shook him even more was the realization that he *wanted* to believe her. "And I don't believe in coincidences."

"What do you believe?" The words were out before Quinn could prevent them.

Abby's gaze locked with his, as if she were trying to decide whether he really wanted to know. And then she nodded once—and smiled—as if she'd gotten the answer. "That God has a plan—a purpose—for our lives."

The simple response tugged at Quinn's soul in a way he hadn't expected it to.

He did believe that God had a plan—for other people. People who amounted to something. That was the reason, when Quinn turned eighteen, that he'd felt responsible for coming up with one of his own.

In Chicago, no one had known anything about his background. They hadn't known that Mike O'Halloran was drunk more than he was sober. They didn't know Jean O'Halloran had walked out on her husband. Not that Quinn blamed his mother for leaving—it just would have been nice if she'd taken him along.

No one in Chicago was watching, waiting for him to make a mistake that would prove he was destined to "turn out just like his old man."

When Hamlin Security hired him, Quinn felt as if he'd been given the second chance that Abby claimed everyone deserved. His colleagues respected him, his employers trusted him…until circumstances had forced him to return to Mirror Lake.

Ken Raynes, the CEO of a software company, had contracted him to provide personal security for his youngest daughter, Serena, who was being harassed by a former boyfriend. The seventeen-year-old was spoiled and rebellious, a potentially combustible combination. Although it was company policy to keep a professional distance from his clients, Quinn had felt sorry for the girl. Serena's parents didn't have time for her and her friends seemed to come around only when they wanted something.

He'd befriended her. Listened to her problems. And when he discovered Serena was hooked on prescription drugs, Quinn went directly to Ken, hoping her father would get Serena the help she needed. When Serena's family confronted her, not only had she denied ever using drugs, she'd informed her parents that Quinn was the one who'd offered to score some for her if she was interested.

In a perfect world, Quinn's word would have carried more weight than that of a troubled teenager. But he didn't live in a perfect world. Ken Raynes traced Quinn's roots back to Mirror Lake and found Mike O'Halloran. An alcoholic. The town troublemaker. It didn't matter that Quinn had a spotless record.

Quinn wanted Serena to get help, but Ken Raynes, who had political aspirations, didn't want a scandal. The only way to make his family look good was to make Quinn look bad.

Quinn had tried to do the right thing and it cost him his career. Not only that, it had forced him to return to the place where he'd always felt he *didn't* belong.

Was he supposed to believe God had a purpose in that?

"So…" The lilt in Abby's voice nudged Quinn out of the shadows. "What do we do now?"

I have no idea, Quinn wanted to say. Until he realized she was asking about locks for the inn, not his past. Or the condition of his soul. "Tell me what you want and I'll write up an estimate."

"Don't bother with an estimate. I trust you."

Why?

The question ricocheted around Quinn's head. Because she believed he was an answer to prayer?

In the past, he would have deliberately tried to gain Abby's trust. It came with the job. Quinn had found when his clients trusted him, they were more willing to listen to his instructions. Follow his recommendations.

If anything, Quinn knew he should feel relieved—not guilty—that Abby's initial reticence toward him seemed to be fading.

Unless she discovers the reason you've been helping her.

For the first time since Quinn had agreed to Alex Porter's terms, fear skated down his spine as he considered how Abby would react if she discovered the truth.

No more trusting looks. No more heart-stopping smiles….

She won't find out, Quinn told himself.

Alex's PI would figure out who was harassing him and realize there was no threat to Abby. Daniel would come back to finish the cabins and Quinn would return to his real job. Abby would be none the wiser. No harm done.

Now all Quinn had to do was believe it.

"How long have you been in business?" Abby asked.

"About a year. Why?"

Color tinted her cheeks. "I can tell you're in the process of…fixing things up. And you work with Daniel, too. I thought…"

He was an answer to prayer who was having trouble making ends meet.

Quinn tried not to wince. Now it made sense. Why she hadn't peppered him with questions about the reason he was dividing his time between O'Halloran Security and the inn.

Abby's next question confirmed his suspicions.

"Do you require a deposit?" Her slender fingers traced a crescent-shaped gash on the corner of his desk. "For materials?"

Quinn frowned. "That's not necessary."

"But—"

"We can hash out the details later."

"Translation—we can argue about it on the way home." Abby flashed an impish smile.

It wasn't the smile that got to him this time. It was the word *home* that opened the door to a host of images Quinn hadn't known lay buried in his subconscious.

What was more unsettling was that he'd never experienced the kind of pictures his imagination was painting. They weren't memories of the ramshackle house he'd grown up in a few miles outside of Mirror Lake. These were different— and yet all too familiar.

In his mind's eye, Quinn saw a fire crackling in the great room. A sunlit kitchen with yellow walls. A nest of cushions in the hammock near the deck...and Abby. In every single one.

Quinn pushed the thoughts from his head before they could take root in his heart.

The future was too uncertain. If O'Halloran Security didn't start turning a profit, he would have to sell it and move on. Quinn was already halfway into his two-year plan.

God has a purpose. A plan.

The conversation he'd had with Abby cycled through his mind again.

She believed that God's plan included converting a rustic camp into a bed-and-breakfast.

Quinn didn't know if that were true or not, but he did know one thing.

God's plan for Abby didn't include him.

Chapter Nine

Abby pushed the heels of her hands into the bread dough and heard an air bubble pop.

Quinn had lied to her.

He didn't "hash" out the details on the drive back to the lodge. He didn't argue about them, either. Because in order to do those things, a person had to be willing to *talk* first. And Quinn hadn't.

Abby didn't count two growls and a harrumph as meaningful conversation.

When they'd arrived back at the inn, Quinn dropped her off at the house and drove down to the cabins. With *her* dog.

She knew he was sensitive about having to work two jobs, although Abby didn't think that was anything to be ashamed of. It proved he wasn't afraid of hard work. That he was committed to making his business succeed.

Come to think of it, they had a lot in common. Quinn would recognize that if he'd put his male pride aside and...

And what?

Smile at you again. Admit it, you want him to like you....

She wasn't going to admit anything. Abby pushed that thought away, only to have another one take its place.

Because you like him.

Over the next hour, three dozen cloverleaf rolls, a chef's salad and a lemon torte formed a line on the counter. Sorting through her recipe card file proved to be much easier than sorting through her feelings for Quinn.

That she even *had* feelings for Quinn was disturbing.

Abby had never been in a serious relationship. In her social circles, she'd never been sure if men were as attracted to her as they were to her last name. And the fortune that went with it.

If, in some rare instance, she did show a spark of interest in someone, Alex swooped in and circled the poor guy like a hawk until he ran for cover.

If a girl mixed those things with a troublesome tendency to be leery of strangers, it added up to a lot of evenings alone.

Not exactly the kind of lifestyle the average person who saw Abby's face on a Porter Hotel brochure would assume she was living.

Although there was a certificate on the wall of her "office" proving she had a business degree, Alex brushed aside her suggestion that he let her take a more active role in the hotels' day-to-day operations.

Six months ago, a feeling of discontent had seeped in. She was tired of being the poster girl for Porter Hotels.

As the corporation's official spokesperson, her face was featured in all the marketing campaigns. A symbol of the type of person who chose to stay at one of their hotels.

Sophisticated. Discriminating. Refined.

Frequent appeals to Alex, asking for more responsibility, fell on deaf ears. He didn't understand her frustration. Tried to assure her that her role as the company spokesperson was important. Abby knew it also served another purpose, although Alex wouldn't have admitted it. It cut down her interaction with people. A billboard was as close as anyone could get to her.

Abby had wanted more. And then she felt guilty for wanting more because she already *had* so much.

Restlessness with life in general drove Abby to her favorite place to reduce stress—the kitchen.

Jessica Benson was the first person who had recognized Abby's restlessness for what it really was. Not a search to "find herself," but to find God. The One who'd created her.

The day Abby surrendered her heart to the Lord and took that first tiny step forward in faith, she hadn't expected to begin a journey that would change the entire landscape of her life.

Skyscrapers for towering white pine. A penthouse apartment for a room tucked under the sloping eaves of a former attic. A small town where people recognized her face—but not because they'd seen it on a billboard. Where they called her by her first name—and weren't intimidated by her last.

Abby had lived in Chicago all her life, but the first time she'd visited Mirror Lake, there had been a heart-to-heart connection.

A place she'd lived for a little over a month now felt like home.

It was no coincidence that she'd found the perfect piece of property to convert into a bed-and-breakfast inn. Or fallen in love with the sleepy little town that curved around the shoreline on the opposite side of the lake.

When doubts crept in, all Abby had to do was look back and count what Jessica called "spiritual signposts." Evidence that she was following the right path. God's path.

The road had its share of potholes, bumps and curves, but

whenever she was discouraged, it seemed as if God was ready with a new signpost.

Like the amazing discovery that Quinn was a locksmith.

Once again, Abby's thoughts moved back to him like a needle seeking North on a compass.

He'd seemed uncomfortable when she'd shown up unexpectedly at his office that afternoon, but Abby understood why.

Kate told her that Quinn had moved back to Mirror Lake a year ago. That would have made it near the time his father had died. Abby didn't have to be a detective to make the connection.

Not only had he inherited Lady, his father's dog, he'd inherited his business.

Abby's respect for him had risen another notch.

What had Quinn given up in order to revive a business that was obviously struggling? What had he left behind?

The questions plagued her as she added a dozen cookies to the already crowded wicker hamper on the table—bait to lure him down from the roof of the cabin.

The sun was setting, and in an hour Quinn would have to hold a flashlight in one hand and a hammer in the other.

Time to send him home.

Shrugging into a lightweight sweater, she grabbed the basket and started across the lawn.

The dogs dozed in the grass. Mulligan's nose twitched as she walked past him, but he made no move to get up.

Abby's initial confidence faded a little as Quinn pushed back the brim of his ball cap and peered down at her.

She could use one of his heart-stopping little half smiles right about now to bolster her courage.

"I brought you a little something."

Quinn's gaze shifted to the picnic basket she'd lugged across the yard. "A little something, huh?"

Abby relaxed when she saw a hint of amusement in his eyes. She'd been afraid he would view it as charity. "All right, there's a lot of little somethings."

Quinn swung down from the ladder and landed right in the middle of her personal space.

Abby's breath stalled when his fingers grazed her palm as he took the basket out of her hand. "Thanks."

"You're welcome."

"Even though I told you that you didn't have to go to any trouble for me."

Come to think of it, he *had* told her that.

"You brought a lot of your food here so I wanted to make sure you had some—" *decent* "—food to tide you over until I see you on Monday."

Quinn stiffened. "Are you going somewhere this weekend?"

"No. You are."

His expression didn't change.

"It's Friday." She tried again. "The day before the weekend. Weekends generally mean time off."

"You're taking the weekend off?"

"Of course not. But I don't expect you to be here 24/7." Abby saw some unidentifiable emotion flare in the depths of his pewter-gray eyes. "*You* have the weekend off."

"I don't need the weekend off."

"I'm giving it to you anyway." She smiled. "You've accomplished more in the past two days than I thought was humanly possible. You earned a break. Besides that, I'm sure you have things of your own to catch up on."

Abby had seen his office. She knew he did.

Quinn wasn't sure how to get past this new complication. "It's covered."

"Well, then—"

"Abby, I don't *want* the weekend off." Quinn waited until he saw understanding dawn in her eyes.

But she only *thought* she understood. And what she thought she understood was that he wanted to work as many hours as possible before Daniel came back.

"You can take Sunday off, then."

Quinn buried a sigh. Abby was determined to give him a day off. Along with a picnic basket loaded with food to pass the time.

"Trying to get rid of me?"

To his amazement, Abby blushed. "N-no."

Once again, Quinn tried to reconcile the woman standing in front of him with the sophisticated woman featured on the billboard advertising Porter Hotels.

It was almost as if there were two Abby Porters. He didn't know which woman was the real Abby Porter, but decided he liked the one with the windswept golden hair and winsome smile better.

"I'd feel guilty if you worked on Sunday," Abby continued. "Because I don't. It's my…rest and refresh day."

Great. Another complication. But thanks to his agreement with Alex Porter, where Abby went, Quinn followed.

"So, what do you do on your rest and refresh day?" He hoped it didn't include shopping. Or socializing.

"In the afternoon, Mulligan and I take a walk around the lake or I try to catch up on some reading…"

Hiking. No problem. He'd tag along. Reading would keep her close to home. It could be worse, Quinn decided. Neither of the things she'd just mentioned involved leaving the property.

"And I go to the early service at Church of the Pines."

"Church of the Pines."

"Have you been there?"

Abby's innocent question opened a floodgate of memories.

As a kid, Quinn had attended Sunday school there one summer. Not long after his mother left, his fourth grade homeroom teacher, Miss Anderson, had pulled him aside and invited him to go to church with her. She drove past their house on Sunday mornings and must have seen him playing outside.

Quinn, willing to grab any opportunity that would take him away from home, had said yes.

There'd been whispers and sidelong glances from the rest of the children when Miss Anderson gently pushed Quinn into the room that first day. They'd subsided when he was put in charge of smoothing tiny felt figures on a flannel board while she told a story about a little man named Zacchaeus, who climbed a tree to see Jesus.

The story stuck in Quinn's mind because no one else liked the man and they wondered why Jesus wanted to go to his house for supper.

Quinn knew exactly how Zacchaeus felt.

After that, he'd looked forward to Sunday mornings. He listened to stories and sang songs he'd never heard before. At snack time, Miss Anderson would put extra crackers on his napkin and refill his glass of juice.

Quinn didn't even mind sitting for another hour in the sanctuary—where the stories were longer and there was nothing to eat. Other kids grumbled and fidgeted if the sermon went longer than it was supposed to, but not Quinn. Sometimes he listened to what the pastor was saying, but most of the time he was content to soak in his surroundings.

The whole room always seemed to be filled with light. Stained glass windows painted rainbows on the gleaming hardwood floors. Tall white candles glowed on a table by the piano.

Quinn had felt safe within the walls.

The stories the pastor told made him feel strong on the inside, too. Quinn had prayed with Miss Anderson one morning and asked Jesus to come into his heart, so he figured that was the reason he felt different. For a little while, he'd imagined it meant that things would *be* different.

They weren't.

Because he always had to go home.

And his father, who was used to Quinn giving him a wide berth, didn't appreciate the change in him.

"Quit pestering me about your ma. I told you, she isn't coming back."

"Yes, she will."

A split second later, Quinn was yanked off his feet.

"Did she tell you that? Did she call you?"

"No." Quinn had gasped the word, wishing he hadn't said anything. In the past, he would have made up a lie. He couldn't this time. Now he knew lying was wrong. *"I've been praying she comes home."*

"Praying?" His father's scornful laugh was somehow more frightening than his rage. *"You think God listens to you?"*

"Miss Anderson said He does."

As soon as he saw his dad's expression, Quinn knew he shouldn't have talked back. Shouldn't have said anything about his teacher. It had only made things worse.

"You've been sneaking out."

"Miss Anderson takes me to church with her."

The laughter faded to a sneer. *"Those people feel sorry for you. You're like a stray mongrel dog they feed once a week so they can feel better about themselves."*

"That's not true." But doubt slithered through Quinn's mind when he remembered the extra crackers Miss Anderson gave him every week.

He tried to remember some of the verses that he'd memorized, the ones Miss Anderson said would give him strength, but Mike O'Halloran had pushed his face close to Quinn's. *"You stick close to home from now on or I'm going to have to pay that pretty schoolteacher of yours a visit. Tell her to mind her own business."*

Quinn had recognized the look in his dad's bloodshot eyes.

The next day at school, he told Miss Anderson he didn't want to go to church anymore. She'd asked him why, but Quinn hadn't told the truth that time. He told her it was boring. To prove his point, he kicked the wastebasket over on his way out the door.

The remainder of the day was spent in the principal's office, waiting for his dad to pick him up. He'd spent the night on the roof, staring up at the heavens. The things his father had said made Quinn wonder if Miss Anderson hadn't gotten it wrong about the kind of people God listened to.

When the snowflakes started to fall, Quinn stopped praying that his mom would come back. By the following summer, he'd stopped praying about anything at all.

"Quinn?"

The light touch of Abby's hand on his arm made him snap to attention. "What?"

She chuckled. "Where did you go?"

"Nowhere." Nowhere he wanted to revisit. And definitely nowhere he would ever take Abby.

But, he thought with an inward sigh, there was somewhere he *would* have to take her.

"I asked if you'd ever gone to church there," Abby reminded him.

"A few times. When I was a kid."

She didn't look surprised. Nor did she ask why he didn't attend anymore. "Do you want to go with me?"

"Sure. Why not?" He didn't have much of a choice so he might as well let her think it was her idea.

A smile backlit Abby's eyes. As if she were genuinely happy he'd agreed to go.

What are You doing, Lord?

The prayer formed in Quinn's soul and took flight before he had a chance to catch it.

It wasn't until later that night, while staring up at the ceiling, Quinn realized he'd actually talked to God again. Asked Him a question.

And now here he was. Lying awake, waiting for an answer.

Chapter Ten

Abby slipped out of the house, a coffee cup in one hand and her walking verse in the other.

Dew glistened in the grass and it was early enough that wisps of fog, soft as cotton candy, hung over the lake.

Mulligan and Lady ran circles around her, ready to go.

"Shh." Abby put a finger to her lips. The shades in the windows of Quinn's cabin were still drawn. "Not everyone likes to get up this early on a Saturday morning, you know."

She hadn't been able to talk Quinn into taking the weekend off but it didn't mean he had to be up and working at the crack of dawn, either.

The dogs streaked ahead and disappeared into the woods. Abby followed at a more leisurely pace, keeping an eye on the grid of roots poking from the ground beneath her feet as she recited the verse out loud.

"'I sought the Lord, and he answered me. He delivered me from all my fears. Those who look to him are radiant.'" Abby peeked at the slip of paper in her hand. "'Their faces are never covered with shame...'"

A branch snapped behind her.

She glanced over her shoulder and saw Quinn closing the distance between them at an easy lope.

There was no escaping the man.

Not that you want to, an inner voice teased.

Before she had time to form a snappy inner comeback, Quinn reached her side.

"What are you doing out here so early?"

Funny, Abby had been about to ask him the same thing.

"I take Mulligan for a walk around the lake every morning," she explained. "Lady followed us again. I hope you don't mind."

"Not a bit." He shrugged. "She's probably happier with the pace you set. I tried to take her with me once, but I ended up carrying her back. We were four miles from home."

Abby pictured Quinn toting the pudgy dog for that distance and laughed. "I won't be offended if you leave us behind in the dust. I've got cinnamon rolls in the oven, so I can only go halfway around this time." She stepped to the side to give him some room, but instead of going on ahead, Quinn fell in step beside her.

"I think you dropped something." He pointed to a piece of paper tumbling down the path in front of them, propelled by a mischievous breeze coming off the lake.

By the time Abby chased it down, she was out of breath. And laughing so hard her ribs ached.

"I admire your dedication to keeping the environment clean," Quinn said when she limped up to him.

"I didn't want to lose it," Abby gasped. "It's my walking verse."

"I'll take your word for it. Because it looked to me like you were running." Quinn's lips curved, a repeat of the rare but potent smile she'd caught a glimpse of the day before.

Abby pressed a hand against the stitch in her side. "Don't make me laugh," she pleaded. "It hurts."

Quinn held out his hand. "Okay. Let's hear it."

"Hear it?"

"Your *walking* verse."

Abby's fingers curled protectively around the piece of paper. "I didn't get much of a chance to look at it." *Before you distracted me.*

"You're stalling." Quinn plucked it from her hand and started down the trail again.

Leaving her with no choice but to follow. "Fine. But you have to start me out."

Quinn looked down at the paper. "'I.'"

Abby made a face at him. "A bigger start."

"'I sought.'"

Abby bumped him with her hip. "Be serious."

He laughed instead.

The sound washed over her—and through her—as warm and unexpected as a summer rain. Bringing the feelings that Abby had been trying to deny into full bloom.

"Sorry." Quinn's laughter faded but a smile continued to dance in his eyes as he looked down at her.

Abby made the mistake of making eye contact with him. The toe of her shoe caught in a root and she pitched forward. Quinn's hand shot out to steady her.

His touch was as warm as his laughter and she was struck by an overwhelming urge to turn into the circle of his arms. Rest her head against his chest.

Whoa. Where did that come from?

She pulled away instead and stumbled up the path, trying to concentrate once more on the verse she'd written down.

"'I sought the Lord, and he answered me. He delivered me

from all my fears. Those who...'" Abby paused, waiting for Quinn to prompt her.

When he didn't, she glanced up at him.

The smile on his face had disappeared, replaced by...disbelief?

Abby's heart sank.

Quinn stared down at the piece of paper, aware that Abby was waiting for him to give her another clue.

He couldn't say a word.

Her "walking verse" was the answer to the question that had cycled through his mind over the course of a sleepless night.

He'd asked God if He was still there. If He was still listening.

I sought the Lord, and he answered me.

Now he understood Abby's reaction the day before when he'd told her that he owned O'Halloran Security. She'd been amazed by what she'd viewed as God's intervention on her behalf.

Quinn was a little amazed himself. So amazed that he couldn't push out another word.

"I'm going to turn around now." Abby's voice intruded softly on his thoughts. "But you can keep going. I don't want to hold you back."

Hold him back? Quinn was beginning to wonder if Abby Porter wasn't responsible for moving him *forward*.

"Did you say something about cinnamon rolls?"

"Yes, I did. But what about your run?"

Quinn shrugged. "I can fit it in later."

"Or..." Abby's eyes held a sparkle of mischief. "I'll race you back." She whirled around and sprinted down the uneven trail.

Once Quinn's initial shock melted away, he started after her. The dogs took up pursuit and all four of them burst into the clearing a few minutes later.

The rusty car parked in the driveway immediately set off Quinn's internal radar. The three teenage boys lounging against the hood looked as questionable as the vehicle.

Abby started in their direction.

"Abby, wait."

She quickened her pace instead. "That's my Saturday painting crew. They're early today. They don't usually show until noon."

The boys intercepted them halfway across the yard but by the time they met, Quinn made sure he got there before Abby.

Abby went down the row, introducing him to Tim and Zach Davis, but hesitated when she got to the third one, a lanky boy who looked to be several years younger than the brothers. He squirmed under her welcoming smile and Quinn had the feeling the kid would have bolted for the car if he hadn't been wedged between the other boys.

"I don't think we've met before," she said.

The boy's dark-eyed gaze couldn't seem to find a place to light. It bounced from Abby to Quinn and back again until it finally settled on the ground.

"This is Cody." Tim finally spoke up. "He wants to paint, too."

"Wonderful." Abby sounded as if she meant it. "This place needs all the help it can get. I know Daniel usually gets you started, but I'll show you the painting supplies—"

"I don't mind playing foreman today," Quinn interrupted. "I know you're anxious to get started on the library."

"I think I'd rather be outside today." Abby tilted her face toward the sun and closed her eyes. "It's going to be a perfect summer day. Beautiful."

When she opened them again, all three teenagers were staring at her.

"What?"

No one said a word. They shuffled and muttered and looked everywhere but at her. Until Quinn intervened. He pointed at the garage. "Thataway. *Boys.*"

With sheepish grins and furtive glances in Abby's direction, they stumbled away.

"Strange." Abby's brow furrowed. "Daniel never mentioned they don't like to talk."

Was Abby really that naive? One smile from her had left them totally tongue-tied.

"That's probably because they talk to him," he said dryly.

"I scared them away, didn't I?" She sighed. "Chalk it up to a lack of experience with kids."

Call him a glutton for punishment, but he wanted to see her smile again. "You could always buy a book."

It worked.

"Maybe I will." Abby grinned. "Right after I finish the one I'm reading on effective communication."

Quinn sucked in a breath.

Maybe it wouldn't be a bad idea to read that one himself.

He knew exactly how the boys had felt. Abby had a way of leaving him tongue-tied, too.

It took all of Abby's willpower to stay inside the lodge and not find a chore to do outside. Other than delivering cold drinks to her work crew, who'd set to work painting the boathouse shortly after their arrival, she'd spent the afternoon in the library.

She planned to turn it into a gathering room, where guests could play board games in the evening or settle into the comfortable chairs with a good book.

Like the other rooms, it boasted a fieldstone fireplace with a raised hearth. A perfect place either to invite conversation or encourage solitude....

Beethoven's *Symphony No. 5* suddenly broke through her musings.

Abby would never feel the same way about classical music again.

"Hi, Alex."

"Change your mind yet?"

"No. Have you?"

It had become their standard greeting over the past few days.

The amusement in Alex's voice, rather than disapproval, gave Abby hope that he was starting to accept her decision.

Abby wasn't sure why, but she'd sensed a change in her brother over the past week. He hadn't been quite as dogged in his attempt to convince her to return to Chicago.

Not that she was complaining. A change like that she could live with. Alex was the only family she had and they'd always been close. The tension between them hadn't been easy to deal with.

"How are things going up there?"

"Great. This has been a productive week." Thanks to Quinn.

"That's good."

"Okay, who are you and what have you done with my brother?"

Alex didn't see the humor in the question. "I only have your best interests at heart."

It was a familiar refrain. One Abby had never been able to argue with. Until now. "Maybe that's part of the problem, Alex. Maybe it's time you followed some of your own interests for a change. You put your life on hold in order to raise your kid sister. But your sister isn't a kid anymore."

She waited for a snappy comeback. There was a reason Alex had been appointed captain of the debate team in college.

"I'm doing what Mom and Dad would want me to do," he finally said.

The hint of uncertainty in Alex's voice tugged at her conscience.

"I know." Abby couldn't argue with that. From the time she was six years old, protecting Abigail Marie had become the Porter family's personal cause. After their parents' death, Alex had continued to carry the torch.

He had to be as tired of bearing that burden as she'd finally become of being the one responsible for it.

"Why don't you come home for the weekend and we'll talk about it."

"I am home."

"I miss you, Abby."

"Now you're inviting me to go on a guilt trip?"

"Is it working?"

She laughed. "You don't give up, do you?"

"You know I don't."

The doorbell came to life, sending out a series of tinny, off-key notes that reminded Abby of a jack-in-the-box.

"I'll call you back later, Alex. There's someone at the door."

"You're going to answer the door?"

"Yes, Alex. I live here," Abby explained patiently. "I'm the logical person to answer the door…." As she pulled it open, the rest of the words died on her lips.

"Who is it?" Alex demanded. "Who's there?"

Abby finally found her voice.

"A police officer."

Chapter Eleven

"I'll call you later, Alex." Abby ignored her brother's squawk of protest as she closed the phone.

The officer swept off his hat, exposing the shiny dome beneath it. "Good afternoon, Miss Porter."

"Good afternoon." Abby opened the door and stepped onto the porch. There was no logical reason for her to be nervous, but the butterflies that took wing inside of her didn't seem to care. "Is there something I can do for you, Officer?"

"Sergeant," he corrected. "Sergeant West. I'm with the county sheriff's department."

"It's nice to meet you, Sergeant. Would you like to sit for a few minutes?" Abby gestured toward the pair of wicker rocking chairs. "I made a pitcher of lemonade this morning, if you'd like a glass."

The deputy cleared his throat. "No, thank you, Miss Porter. I'm here on official business."

Abby's heart dropped to her feet. "What is this about?"

"It's been brought to my attention that Cody Lang is working for you."

Something about the man's tone immediately put Abby on the defensive. "Tim and Zach Davis brought Cody with them today to do some painting. This is the first time I've met him."

"Lang's name came up this past week. We've had a rash of burglaries in some of the cabins on the other side of the lake. The sheriff's department has good reason to think he was involved."

"But you aren't sure."

The deputy's eyes narrowed. Maybe he heard something he didn't like in *her* tone. "My source is usually reliable. When there's trouble, it's a safe bet one of the Lang boys is in the middle of it. It looks like this one is following his brother's footsteps."

"I'm sure Cody will be all right. He's just looking for a chance to earn some extra money like other boys his age."

"Or he wanted to check things out." Sergeant West shrugged. "If I were you, I'd send him on his way, not give him the run of the place."

Goose bumps rose on Abby's arms. "I appreciate your concern but Zach and Tim vouched for Cody and he seems like a polite boy—" in spite of his inability to look her in the eyes "—and since you don't have proof that he was involved in the burglaries, I think I'll keep him on, at least for today. I have more than enough to keep him busy."

Stereo speakers suddenly launched an attack of pounding bass, drowning out the birdsong in the trees.

Perfect timing, boys, Abby thought.

Sergeant West's gaze swung toward the lake, locking on the four figures near the dock. "I understand O'Halloran is staying with you."

Abby stiffened. Apparently the officer had more than one reliable source. "I'm on a tight deadline. Mr. O'Halloran is able to put in longer days if he stays in one of the *cabins*."

She put some weight on the last word, just in case there was any confusion as to where Quinn was staying.

"How is that going?"

"He's making a lot of progress—"

"That's not what I meant," the sergeant interrupted, not taking his eyes off Quinn. "Does he…keep to himself?"

Abby frowned. She didn't understand the question but she didn't appreciate his tone. "I thought you drove out here to check on Cody Lang."

"Like I said, you haven't lived in Mirror Lake long enough to be privy to certain…information."

"Or swayed by prejudice."

Sergeant West's gaze swung back to her. "Mike O'Halloran, Quinn's father, was bad news. Everybody around here knows it."

Abby had noticed the way Quinn's expression hardened whenever he spoke of his father. For the first time, she had some insight into the reason why.

"I thought we were talking about Quinn."

The officer shrugged, as if that detail didn't matter. "Same family."

"Different men." Abby dug her nails into her palms to stop her hands from shaking.

"The apple doesn't fall far from the tree, so the saying goes."

Abby had only known Quinn for a few days, but she knew it didn't apply to him, no matter what his father had been guilty of.

"I'll keep that in mind," she said politely. "Thank you for stopping by, Sergeant."

The officer gave her a sharp look, as if judging her sincerity. "You keep an eye on Lang. If he causes any trouble, let me know." Sergeant West's gaze strayed to Quinn again. "Something else you might keep in mind, Miss Porter. A man who doesn't talk about his past…well, he usually has a reason."

Quinn watched the squad car pull away.

The tension in Abby's shoulders told him the deputy hadn't stopped by for a social call.

"What do you think he wanted?"

Quinn glanced at Cody Lang, wondering if the boy had read his mind. The kid looked a little tense himself; the hunted look in his dark eyes all too familiar.

The boy's last name wasn't familiar but then again, Quinn had been gone a long time. It was possible the Lang family had migrated to the area after he'd left town.

"I don't know." But he planned to find out.

"She looks upset," Cody whispered.

Quinn thought so, too, but he was surprised by the intuitive comment. He glanced at Cody and saw the raw fear banked in his eyes before he averted his gaze.

The kid must have come to his own conclusion as to why the deputy had stopped by to talk to Abby.

"You tell Tim and Zach that break time is over, okay?" Quinn planned to give Cody a light, reassuring cuff on the shoulder but when his hand came up, the boy flinched.

Quinn silently berated himself. He should have known better.

"I'll be back in a few minutes."

Lost in thought, Abby didn't seem to be aware of his approach.

Quinn's vow to keep a professional distance disintegrated when he saw Abby's hands clenched at her sides.

Had the deputy delivered bad news?

"Problem?" He tossed out the question to let Abby know he was there.

She thought he'd been teasing the day before, when he called out a greeting to warn her of his presence. He hadn't been. Abby's vague response that day in the chapel when he'd asked why she had read a book on self-defense techniques still chewed at the edge of his thoughts.

"Not anymore."

"Sergeant West."

"You know him?"

"I remember him." An answer that wasn't quite an answer, but it was the best Quinn could do. The deputy had been fresh out of the academy when he was a kid. "I'm not surprised he stopped by to say hello. He likes to keep tabs on things." Which probably explained why the deputy hadn't retired yet.

"He didn't stop by to say hello," Abby said. "He heard Cody Lang was here. It sounds like Cody was implicated in some burglaries that happened a few days ago. Cabins on the other side of the lake. Sergeant West wanted to make sure I was aware of it."

It had been fear he'd seen on Cody's face, not guilt, but he didn't think that would matter to Abby. If West pegged the boy as a suspect, Abby would believe him.

His jaw tightened. "Do you want me to tell Cody?"

"Tell him what?" Abby looked up at him, a question in her eyes.

"That you want him to leave?"

"Why would you do that? I need him," Abby shocked him by saying. "And there's no proof Cody was one of the boys who broke into the cabins."

Laughter rolled across the lawn as the Davis brothers began to wrestle in the grass like a pair of frisky puppies. Quinn noticed that Cody was still staring in their direction, as if he knew they were talking about him.

"There's no proof he wasn't involved, either," Quinn pointed out.

Doubt surfaced in Abby's expressive eyes. He could almost read her thoughts.

Maybe the sergeant was right. He could be checking out the place to see if there's anything worth coming back for. When you're alone…

"Cody will understand," Quinn said. "In fact, he's probably expecting it."

Abby's chin lifted, as if in answer to an unspoken question. "Don't say anything to him."

"Are you sure?"

"I'm sure."

"What about Sergeant West?"

"What about him? He was just doing his job. Warning me about Cody." Abby started across the yard.

Quinn caught up to her in less than a stride.

"What else did he warn you about?"

Quinn's tone was even; it was the bleak look in his eyes that stopped Abby in her tracks.

He knew.

Maybe, like Cody, he'd also expected it.

If Sergeant West hadn't made that disparaging comment about Quinn's father, Abby might have missed the shadow that skimmed across his face.

Had Quinn experienced the same kind of mistrust? Judgment?

Part of the reason Abby loved the idea of living in a small town was because of the "everyone knows your name" charm it represented. She hadn't thought of that in terms of the negative.

She sensed that Quinn was waiting for her answer.

"He thought he should fill me in on a little area history." Abby's indignation, on simmer, began to bubble up again as she recalled the conversation with Sergeant West.

"And how it repeats itself." It wasn't a question.

Abby took another step forward but Quinn's hand caught her wrist.

She didn't pull away, although she could have. Quinn wasn't holding her captive. His grip was too loose, too gentle, for that.

How could she explain that she knew what it felt like to have people make assumptions based on her family? On her last name?

It had happened all the time. As the "face" of Porter Hotels, some people had treated her as if she didn't have a brain. Assumed she had a personality as shallow as the piece of paper the brochure was printed on.

"I prefer to make up my own mind," she finally said. "Based on what I see, not what people say."

Quinn stared down at her, searching for the truth. "And what do you see?"

They weren't talking about Cody anymore.

Quinn hadn't let go of her wrist. Without thinking, Abby squeezed his hand. His eyes darkened and his fingers closed around hers...

"Miss Porter?"

They jerked apart as Cody sidled up. His gaze riveted on his feet. "I wanted to say thanks. For letting me paint today."

Abby felt a rush of compassion. It was obvious from the set of the boy's narrow shoulders that he expected to be sent on his way. So he'd decided to leave on his own to save himself more embarrassment.

She pretended not to understand. "Do you have to go now?"

Cody looked taken aback by the question. "I—I thought you'd want me to," he mumbled.

"Actually, I've got another job for you. If you're interested."

Cody's shoulder lifted and fell. "I don't have anything else to do."

Abby wasn't fooled by the casual tone or the matching shrug. He knew the reason Sergeant West stopped by and was doing his best to hold his tattered pride together.

"I want to try out a new recipe but in order to do that, I need some fish," she said briskly. "I was having pretty good luck last weekend casting for sunfish in those lily pads at the end of the dock. Are you willing to give it a try? I'll pay you for your time."

"You're going to pay me? To fish?" Cody's voice thinned out and cracked on the last word, reminding her, for all his forced bravado, how young he was.

"It's something that needs to be done and I don't have time to do it." Abby mustered a stern look at having her motives questioned. "So, what do you say?"

Cody darted an "is this for real" look at Quinn. What he saw must have reassured him because a wide grin split his face.

"I say yes."

"Ask Zach and Tim if they want to help. There are enough fishing poles in the storage shed for all three of you."

"Okay. I'll tell them." Cody backed up three steps, turned around and sprinted across the yard as if he were afraid Abby might change her mind.

"They'll be here all evening now," Quinn predicted.

"I know." Abby couldn't help sounding a bit smug. But Cody's expression was worth an adjustment in her plans.

"They're not going to get another thing accomplished the rest of the afternoon."

"I know."

"And they're going to tell all their friends that Abby Porter pays her employees to fish." Quinn sighed. "But I guess it doesn't matter what I think. You're the boss."

"You're right. And because I'm the boss, I can order you to supervise them."

Quinn tunneled his hand through his hair and gave her an impatient look. "I've got work to do."

"Yes, you do." Abby pressed her lips together to flatten a smile.

He spotted it anyway. "Abby—"

"Boss." She tapped an index finger against her chest.

"Bossy, you mean," Quinn muttered. "You're determined to give me some time off this weekend, one way or another, aren't you?"

Apparently nothing got past the man!

"I have no idea what you mean," Abby denied primly.

"Uh-huh." He didn't look convinced.

She sensed Quinn was going to continue the argument, but the series of whoops erupting from the Davis brothers told her that Cody had relayed the news about the change in their job description.

"I better show them where everything is." Abby chuckled. "And they *do* need supervision. I have no idea how to harness that kind of energy."

Quinn fell into step with her. He didn't even have to touch her and every nerve ending in Abby's body began to hum in response to his closeness.

"What made you decide that Cody wasn't involved in the break-ins?" he said after a moment.

Abby slanted a look at him. Nothing in Quinn's expression gave away his thoughts, but she sensed that her answer was important.

She told the truth.

"I didn't."

Chapter Twelve

"Look at this one, Abby!" Cody called, holding up a bluegill the size of Quinn's hand.

"It's definitely a keeper."

Quinn heard Abby's lilting voice and glanced over his shoulder. She was making her way down to the dock, balancing a tray loaded with snacks.

He was beginning to think she had a kitchen full of elves that did all her baking.

"Is anyone hungry?"

The three boys immediately abandoned their fishing poles, with Cody Lang leading the stampede toward the picnic table.

Quinn had a feeling the younger boy craved attention more than food.

The change he'd seen in Cody over the past two hours was startling. With every fish he caught—and brought to Quinn for approval—a glimmer of pride had begun to burn away his initial wariness like sunlight pushing its way through a storm cloud.

Quinn had no doubt the credit for the boy's transformation belonged to Abby. In spite of her claim not to understand kids, she'd somehow managed to come up with the perfect plan to convince Cody to stay. With his pride still intact.

He'd been wrestling with the fact that, in spite of her misgivings, she hadn't sent the kid on his way with Sergeant West's blessing.

And asked you to go along.

Quinn released a quiet breath.

What had the deputy said about him?

The rose tint blooming in Abby's cheeks affirmed that West hadn't missed an opportunity to fill her in on what she'd tactfully referred to as "local history."

I believe what I see. Not what people say.

Abby's response should have put Quinn's mind at ease, not given birth to a dozen more questions.

"There's plenty." Abby waved at him. "At least there is now. I can't guarantee if that will be true in five minutes."

Quinn, who'd found a loose plank on the dock to fix while the boys fished, raised the hammer in response to her invitation. "I'll be right there."

"You snooze, you lose!" Zach Davis shouted.

Abby's laughter followed the teenager's challenge and it was all Quinn could do not to roll his eyes when he saw the shy but adoring looks the boys cast her way. It was clear she'd won them over—and not just with her cooking skills.

Quinn watched her fill glasses of lemonade, chatting easily as if they'd known each other for years.

It was possible that her self-proclaimed ignorance of knowing how to relate to kids was actually working to her advantage. She didn't try to win them over.

Abby was just being…Abby.

Friendly. Generous. Hospitable.

It occurred to Quinn that she possessed all the qualities of a great innkeeper. She had a way of making people feel…welcome. Accepted.

The first conversation he'd had with Alex Porter pushed its way, unbidden, into Quinn's mind. Abby's brother didn't think she was capable of running a bed-and-breakfast. In fact, Quinn had gotten the distinct impression Alex didn't think Abby was capable of much of anything.

He'd described her as fragile.

Quinn hadn't thought much about it at the time, other than to add that particular trait to the list of reasons why he shouldn't have accepted Alex's proposition. He assumed that no one would know better than one of Abby's own family members what she was, or wasn't, capable of doing.

But over the past few days, without Quinn even being fully aware of it, the sophisticated figurehead of Porter Hotels had gradually started to be replaced by…Abby. A woman who tackled difficult projects with a gleam of determination in her eyes and a how-to book in her hand. A woman with a smile that shimmered like sunlight on water. A woman whose faith wasn't the cardboard kind—it was the wide-eyed, childlike kind that expected God to do amazing things.

Didn't Alex see any of those qualities?

One of them was dead wrong about her and Quinn was beginning to have an unsettling feeling that it wasn't him….

"Last piece of chocolate cake!" Abby ignored the chorus of protests as she held the plate above her head—and out of the boys' reach.

Quinn rose to his feet, reluctant to join them. His crowded thoughts didn't leave much room for making polite conversation. He didn't have Abby's talent for putting people at ease.

Cody scooted over on the bench to make room for him. A smear of chocolate frosting bracketed his mouth and Quinn plucked a cloth napkin out of the basket and handed it to him.

"Thanks," Cody mumbled around a mouthful of cake.

From there, the conversation dwindled as the teenagers got serious in their attempt to sample everything on the tray.

Abby filled a glass and handed it to him, the smile on her face reflected in her eyes. Eyes that didn't hold a smidge of doubt or suspicion. Wisps of sun-streaked hair had escaped the apple-green bandana on her head. The color matched the patchwork apron tied around her waist.

She looked totally...*kissable.*

The piece of cake Quinn had just swallowed lodged in his throat.

"I see you found the loose board on the dock."

Abby's words buzzed in his ears like a tree full of cicadas. Great. He was acting like the rest of the adolescent boys at the table!

"Actually, it found me." The board had cracked beneath his weight when he'd stepped on it.

"I caught some nice perch." Zach gulped the remainder of his lemonade and reached for the pitcher.

Abby beat him to it and refilled his glass.

"So did Cody," Tim chimed in.

Cody's ears turned red. "They were okay."

"I can't wait to try them." Abby put one hand on Cody's shoulder.

Quinn saw him shrink from her touch and wondered if Abby had noticed.

Tim snagged the last slice of watermelon from the bowl. "We have to go pretty soon. We're taking our grandma out for dinner tonight."

"Yeah." Tim sighed. "If she doesn't eat right at six-thirty, she says it messes up her constitution. Whatever that is."

"But we can come back tomorrow," Zach added, his expression hopeful.

Over the boy's head, Quinn aimed a what-did-I-tell-you look at Abby.

She crossed her eyes.

Quinn choked.

Tim leaned over and obligingly thumped him on the back.

"I don't think tomorrow will work out," Abby said. "There's church in the morning and I'm afraid I have plans for the rest of the afternoon."

Silence fell, along with the boys' faces.

Abby tilted her head thoughtfully. "But why don't you call me on Monday? I'm sure Quinn and I can come up with a few other things for you to do this week."

That, and the fact that Abby passed around the plate of cookies again, cheered them up.

"Come on, Code." Tim rose to his feet and snaked an arm around Cody's neck, seizing him in an affectionate headlock as he pulled him off the bench.

Abby discreetly doled out white envelopes to each boy as they got up to leave. "Thank you for all your hard work today."

All three nodded and shuffled their feet. And blushed. Then they trooped away, pushing and jostling each other with every step.

"Are boys always like that?" Abby whispered.

"Like what?"

"In perpetual motion."

"You have a brother."

"Alex was never like that." Abby sounded certain as she began to gather up the dishes. "He was seriously…serious."

"I should clean the fish they caught." Quinn wouldn't have minded, except that Sergeant West's visit had made him start thinking about getting those locks changed. "You might not have noticed they didn't get around to that part of the job."

"They didn't have time." Abby winked. "Because of Grandma's, um, constitution."

The impact of that mischievous wink shot through Quinn like a lightning bolt and left him reeling. While he tried to recover from the impact, a car horn blasted.

Abby twisted around, lifting her hand to wave goodbye. Her face clouded. "I think something's wrong."

Quinn turned in the direction of the driveway and saw Cody loping back.

"Zach's car won't start," he gasped once he was within earshot.

"I'll take a look at it." Quinn should have known Abby would follow. Mulligan and Lady, curious over what the fuss was about, trailed along, too.

Twenty minutes later, after Quinn had pronounced the engine dead, the boys circled the ancient Impala like mourners at a graveside service.

"I can't get ahold of Dad. He's not answering the phone," Tim complained. "They must be waiting for us at the restaurant."

"Grandma has a rule against using our cell phones in the restaurants," Zach explained. "She makes Dad turn his off, too."

"That's okay…" Abby looked at Quinn.

He couldn't read minds but somehow he knew what she was going to say next.

"I'm sure Quinn can drop you off."

Yup. That was exactly what he knew she would say.

And he had no way to get out of it. He couldn't suggest

she ride along because there wasn't room in his truck—or her convertible—for the five of them.

Silently, he figured out how much time it would take to run the Davis brothers back to Mirror Lake and drop off Cody at home. A half hour. Tops. Quinn weighed that against the possibility of Alex calling for an update on Abby's location.

"Sure. No problem."

The boys piled into Quinn's pickup and he gave them a moment to adjust before he squeezed into the front cab next to Cody. At least the dogs hadn't tried to hitch a ride.

The last thing Quinn saw when he looked in the rearview mirror was Abby. Laughing.

"You're meeting your family at the Grapevine Café, right?" Quinn asked once they were on the road.

"Nope." Zach shook his head. "The Cedars."

Quinn's back teeth ground together.

The Cedars was located ten miles west of Mirror Lake. It would add another half hour onto the trip.

Abby will be fine, Quinn reminded himself. There was still a good hour of daylight left.

He tried not to think about the break-ins across the lake but put a little more pressure on the gas pedal, hoping Sergeant West wasn't running radar on one of the side roads.

Zach and Tim's parents appeared the moment Quinn's truck pulled up by the front door of the restaurant, resulting in another delay. Quinn spent five minutes explaining who he was and why he'd given the boys a ride and another five minutes offering their father a possible diagnosis as to what was wrong with the car.

Forty-five minutes later, he turned down the private road that wound through an archway of maple and oak to the lodge.

The first thing Quinn noticed was that the house was dark. That in itself struck him as odd. The moment the sun began to set, Abby turned on every light until the place glowed like a Chinese lantern.

Quinn parked the truck by the cabin and got out. The peach and pink sunset spilled from the horizon onto the lake as if someone had tipped over a paint can. Everything was calm. Quiet.

Too quiet.

There was no sign of Abby. Or Lady and Mulligan.

Quinn's next breath stayed in his lungs.

Because what he did see was a ribbon of black smoke curling over the roof of the lodge.

It wasn't working.

Abby cupped one hand over her mouth and, with the other, tossed another handful of sticks into the ring of stones.

According to the book there were supposed to be flames, not smoke.

"What am I doing wrong?" she murmured.

Lady and Mulligan, who'd camped a safe distance away from the fire pit and were sharing one of Abby's homemade biscuits, both stopped chewing and raised their heads.

But they weren't looking at her.

Abby turned her head just in time to see Quinn round the corner of the house. At a full run.

She vaulted to her feet, startled by the wild look in his eyes and half expecting to see a black bear at his heels.

Dread bloomed in Abby's chest. She couldn't imagine what would rattle a man like Quinn.

Had he seen something?

Someone?

As much as she'd tried to put it out of her mind, Deputy West's warning about the break-ins had whittled away at her confidence. After Quinn had left with the boys, she'd needed something to prevent fear from highjacking her inner peace.

The thought of taking a walk to the chapel wasn't as appealing as it usually was, which discouraged Abby even more. She wanted to enjoy God's creation, not worry about vandals using the woods as a hiding place.

She'd decided to tackle one of the projects on her to-do list until Quinn came back.

The expression on his face, however, drained away her initial relief at his return.

"What's wrong?" She was almost afraid to ask.

He skidded to a stop a few feet away from her. "Saw. Smoke."

She frowned, because it looked as if he were having trouble breathing. Which didn't make sense given the fact that *she* was the one whose lungs had been seared by the smoke!

"I know." Abby coughed. "But it's supposed to be a fire."

Quinn looked at her. And the fire pit. And then he dropped to the ground and covered his face with his hands.

Strange.

"Are you all right?"

"Yes." His teeth snapped together on the word.

"You don't look fine. You look…upset. Did something happen?"

He lifted his head, peering at her through narrowed eyes. "Apparently not."

Not sure how to interpret that, Abby picked up a sturdy branch and poked at one of the logs. Another cloud of smoke billowed into the air.

"What are you doing?"

Abby would have thought it was obvious.

"Making a campfire. And believe me. It's not as easy as it looks in the picture."

"Picture."

Maybe, Abby thought, she shouldn't have mentioned the picture. But it was too late. Quinn was already reaching for the manual, facedown on the grass and open to page thirty-four.

He squinted at the camouflage cover and read the title out loud. *"How to Survive and Thrive in the Woods."*

Something in his tone put her on the defensive. "There's a really interesting chapter on edible plants, too."

Quinn set the book down. Carefully. "Why are you making a campfire?"

"Because…" Abby wasn't sure she wanted to confess it was because she'd read that an evening campfire was considered standard entertainment for any respectable country bed-and-breakfast. "The guests are going to expect a campfire. For sing-alongs. Roasting marshmallows. I figured I better practice so I don't embarrass myself."

Well, in front of anyone else, Abby silently amended. It was too late for that with Quinn.

She was thankful the shadows hid her face. She couldn't blame the heat in her cheeks on her pitiful attempt to start a fire. Once again, discouragement punched holes in her confidence and drained away some of the initial enthusiasm she'd felt while following the step-by-step directions in the manual.

"I know. I'm a city mouse in the country." Abby's attempt at humor fell flat. She fiddled with the knot at her waist where she'd tied the tails of her shirt together.

"You don't look like a city mouse." Quinn's gaze swept over her and Abby cringed.

She could only imagine what she looked like. Her faded cutoff jeans and denim shirt were more white than blue. She'd stuffed her bandana in her back pocket when it got snagged in a branch—the same branch that didn't want to let go of her hair when she'd searched for sticks to burn.

"You look more like…Huckleberry Finn."

"Thank you." Abby smiled.

"Most women wouldn't take that as a compliment." He rose fluidly to his feet and studied the smoldering logs.

"That's good. I don't think I want to be *most women.*"

"You're not." A reluctant smile tugged at Quinn's lips.

She took that as a compliment, too.

"The book doesn't say you have to use dry wood, not green," he said after a moment. "You wouldn't know that by looking at a picture."

There was not an ounce of condescension in his voice.

"Oh." Abby didn't know why, but that made her feel a little better. A smile tipped her lips. "So maybe I *can* survive and thrive in the woods?"

Quinn's gaze shifted back to her.

"I think…" He paused and Abby braced herself to accept his criticism. "That Abby Porter can survive and thrive anywhere."

Chapter Thirteen

Quinn couldn't believe he'd said the words out loud. But he must have, because Abby lit up like a Fourth of July sparkler.

His pulse, which had finally started to even out after discovering the source of the smoke, picked up speed again.

That was his cue to leave. Retreat. *Escape*.

Maybe a few hours of sleep would restore the ten years that had been stripped from his life when he'd seen the smoke and thought Abby's house was on fire.

Somehow, he doubted it.

Four years in the U.S. Marines and seven as a bodyguard with one of the most prestigious personal security firms in the Midwest and he'd practically collapsed in the dirt at the bright yellow daisies on Abby's sandals.

Practically? An inner voice gibed.

Okay, he *had* collapsed in the dirt at the bright yellow daisies on Abby's sandals.

That was another thing Quinn couldn't explain. He'd been in dangerous situations before, but his knees had never turned to liquid the way they had when he'd spotted Abby, safe and sound by the fire pit.

Quinn wasn't sure if he could thank Sergeant West or Alex Porter for his overreaction to a nonexistent threat. What he *was* sure of was that he wouldn't get any sleep until Abby was in the house for the night.

"The fire will go out on its own," he said. "There isn't much of a breeze tonight, so the sparks shouldn't be a problem."

Abby kicked at one of the logs with the toe of her shoe, a thoughtful look on her face.

"Good night." Quinn waited for her to take the hint.

"'Night." Abby dusted her palms against her jeans. And glanced toward the woods.

He should have known. "Let's go."

"Go where?"

Quinn knew he was going to regret this.

"To find some dry wood."

"No wonder people like campfires. I didn't understand it until now."

Not content simply to prove that she could start a campfire, Abby had settled down to enjoy it, too. She leaned forward, holding her palms out to capture the heat. The firelight played over her features, turning her porcelain complexion to gold.

Quinn cast a longing look in the direction of his cabin and lowered himself onto one of the wool trapper blankets Abby had spread out next to the fire instead.

For a few minutes, the only sound was an occasional snap as the flames spread through the kindling.

Abby put a hand over her mouth to stifle a yawn. And failed.

"You're tired." Quinn wasn't surprised. She rose at dawn and lights glowed in the windows of the lodge well past midnight.

"Yes." Another yawn slipped out. "But I don't want to move." She drew the corners of the blanket over her legs and scooted closer to the edge of the stones. A blissful smile stretched across her face. "This feels too good."

Quinn silently agreed. Which was another reason to call it a night.

"I should clean the fish the boys caught." He'd had to put that task aside in order to play chauffeur. "We have to get up early for church, right?" he added, hoping Abby would take his second not-so-subtle hint.

Across the fire, he saw her catch her lower lip between her teeth.

"What?"

"I, um, let the fish go."

"You…" Quinn couldn't have heard her right.

"Let them go. They were still alive when I pulled the stringer out of the water so I thought—"

"You'd give them another chance," Quinn finished.

"So they could get a little bigger."

Unbelievable. But so…Abby.

"I am not going to tell the boys what you did." Quinn smiled and heard Abby catch her breath. He frowned. "Cold?"

Mutely, she shook her head. Drawing her legs up against her chest, she rested her chin on her knees and met his gaze across the fire.

Uh-oh.

Quinn had been afraid of this. The intimate warmth of a campfire didn't only lend itself to sing-alongs and s'mores. Like a quiet nook in shadowy, candlelit corner of a restaurant, a campfire also created an optimal environment for conversation.

For *sharing.*

Exactly the kind of thing he'd promised himself that he would avoid when it came to this assignment.

"Do you think Cody will be all right?"

The question took him by surprise. Although it shouldn't have. Abby, who didn't know if the boy she'd fussed over that afternoon was guilty of breaking and entering, had fussed over him anyway.

Unfortunately, Quinn couldn't give her any guarantees. "He has Zach and Tim looking out for him."

"Do you know anything about his family? Sergeant West said something about him following in his brother's footsteps."

Apparently, Sergeant West had had a lot to say during his ten-minute conversation with Abby.

"I don't know anything about the Langs," Quinn said truthfully. He could make a few guesses—none that would guarantee Abby a good night's sleep, however.

"Do you think Cody was involved? In the break-ins?"

"No." Although Quinn wouldn't have been surprised to find out the boy knew the names of the people who were.

He decided not to mention that, either, but Abby must have drawn her own conclusions because her eyes darkened with concern.

Not wanting her to worry that her cabins might be a future target, Quinn tried to think of something to put her mind at ease.

"I'm planning to put the new locks in on Monday. If my boss gives me a thumbs-up, that is."

As he'd hoped, a smile worked the corner of Abby's lips. "I suppose so. As long as you don't shirk your other duties."

His other duties.

Quinn closed his eyes briefly at the innocent reminder.

It was becoming too easy to forget what those "other duties" were when they were together.

"Quinn?"

His eyes snapped open. Abby was leaning forward. This time, the concern in her eyes was for him.

"You can't even keep your eyes open." She clucked her tongue. "I'll see you in the morning."

Quinn should have been relieved she'd finally decided to turn in for the night…except for one nagging detail. While she was eager to send him on his way, she'd scooped up the manual and begun to page through it.

There was no telling what she was planning this time.

"I'm not that tired." He crossed his arms behind his head and got comfortable. "In fact, I think I'm getting my second wind."

Abby's heart did a somersault when Quinn unfolded his lean frame next to the fire.

In spite of what she'd said earlier, her reluctance to retire for the night wasn't only because she didn't want to leave the warmth of the fire. She didn't want to leave Quinn, either.

As guarded as he could be, once again she'd witnessed his softer side when he'd interacted with Cody and the Davis brothers that afternoon.

She hadn't been spying on them, but the library windows did overlook the lake, after all.

Abby had seen Quinn patiently untangling Cody's fishing line. Pausing in his work to admire the latest catch. Laughing at the boys' antics.

No matter what Quinn's father had been like, she knew without a doubt that Sergeant West was wrong about Quinn. Quinn's actions affirmed the kind of man he was.

When he'd returned and witnessed the disaster of a fire she'd made, he hadn't made her feel like an idiot. Or taken control of the situation, the way Alex would have.

I think Abby Porter can survive and thrive anywhere.

While she'd struggled to absorb that astonishing—and unexpected—compliment, Quinn had led her into the woods, showed her which kind of wood burned the best and then left her alone to find it. When she met him back at the fire pit with an armload of birch, Abby felt like a prospector who'd struck gold. Not only because she'd managed to start a respectable campfire, but because of Quinn.

There was no denying it. She was drawn to him. And not just physically, although his rugged good looks were incredibly easy on the eyes. She was drawn to his strength, which made her feel safe rather than vulnerable. To the sense of humor that surfaced at unexpected times and made her laugh.

She didn't feel pressure to have to conform to certain expectations when she was with him. Abby had found few people she could be herself with and it was a little unnerving to discover that Quinn, in the space of a few short days, had become one of them.

Abby glanced up and found him watching her. The intensity of his gaze made her wonder what he was thinking.

Quinn seemed to have an uncanny way of knowing her thoughts so she quickly averted her gaze and tossed a handful of pine needles into the blaze.

"Now that I know how to make a fire, I think I'm going to start one every night. This is a very nice way to end a day." *You're rambling again, Abby,* she chided herself. Knowing that, however, didn't make it any easier to stop! "It's like a little piece of paradise here. I'm not surprised you came back to Mirror Lake."

"I didn't plan to."

Abby couldn't believe she'd heard him right. "I thought you came back to take over your father's business."

"I came back to sell it."

The words hung in the air between them. As tempting as it was to push, to ask Quinn why he'd changed his mind and stayed, Abby waited.

Would he trust her?

"The veteran's hospital called to tell me that Dad's liver and kidneys were failing," he said at length. "I didn't know he was that sick. Whenever I called, he wouldn't talk to me more than a few minutes. By the time I got there, he'd slipped into a coma. Two hours later, he was gone."

Abby felt her heart wrench as Quinn paused, knowing he was reliving that moment.

Her mind flashed back to a hospital waiting room. Alex had walked in, his face a pale canvas, shaded with gray. He'd reached for her and she'd instinctively backed away, as if she could escape the truth of what he was about to say.

Both of them. Gone.

"I know what that's like," she murmured. "Not to have a chance to say goodbye. There are things you wish you could have said. Things you wish you would have done. I'm sure your father felt the same way."

"You didn't know my father."

There it was again. The tension in Quinn's jaw. The bleak look in his eyes.

Mike O'Halloran was bad news. Everyone around here knew it.

"What was he like?"

"Sergeant West didn't tell you?"

Abby caught her breath at the challenging look in his eyes. It was almost as if he'd read her thoughts.

"I'd rather hear it from you," she said simply.

"The story isn't all that unique." Quinn shrugged. "Dad spent more time at the tavern than he did at home. He liked whiskey because it made him feel powerful. But all that meant was that he had the strength to break things. Furniture. Dishes. His business." A pause. "People."

The shuttered look on his face warned Abby not to feel sorry for him.

His story might not be unique, she thought, but that didn't mean it hadn't been an incredibly difficult one for a child to live out.

Alex had taken care of her after their parents died. Who had been there for Quinn? He hadn't mentioned his mother, leaving Abby to assume that she hadn't been a significant part of his life.

"I'd left Mirror Lake after graduation and hadn't planned to come back. When I found out how sick Dad was, I had to. He didn't have anyone else."

He made it sound so simple but Abby knew it must have been difficult to come back. Even more difficult to stay, if people shared Sergeant West's opinion about his family.

From what Quinn had told her, his father hadn't been there for him. And yet he hadn't let that determine his actions. Abby wondered if Quinn realized what that said about his character.

A log collapsed, sending a shower of sparks into the air.

Quinn didn't seem to notice.

"Like I said, I got there too late. After he died, I inquired about arrangements and found out it had already been done. He didn't even need me for that." Quinn shook his head. "I also found out that, for some reason that only made sense to him, Dad had left everything to me. A house on the verge of foreclosure. A business about to go bankrupt."

The undercurrent of bitterness in his voice told Abby that he hadn't welcomed the news.

"But you accepted the challenge. You stayed in Mirror Lake."

"I didn't have much of a choice. A week before Dad died, I…lost my job." Quinn shifted, as if to dislodge the memories pressing in on him. "When I found out he'd left everything to me, it was as if he had the last laugh. Like having someone toss you an anchor when you're out in the middle of the lake, treading water."

Abby moistened her lips. Quinn's body language warned her that he wouldn't welcome someone else's perspective on the matter but she had to obey to a soft, inner prompting.

"Your dad might not have had your best interests at heart, but you have a heavenly Father who loves you and He does," Abby said softly, feeling her way. Praying for wisdom. "Maybe inheriting the business wasn't an anchor meant to drag you down. Maybe it was God's way of giving you a lifeline."

Chapter Fourteen

The aroma of freshly brewed coffee swept over Quinn the moment he reached the deck.

He'd already gone through half a pot but wouldn't turn down another cup. The caffeine surfing through his veins was the only thing lifting the fog from his brain.

The conversation he'd had with Abby had gone through his mind so many times during the night that it had worn a permanent rut there.

He hadn't meant to talk about his father. Especially with Abby. Opening up the door to his past was dangerous on more than one level, for both of them. Before he realized what was happening, he'd let it slip that he had lost his former job. If Abby hadn't been focused on Quinn's relationship with his father, she could have questioned him about where he'd lived. What he'd done for a living.

Not only had Abby managed to sneak through his defenses, once she'd gotten through, she'd dropped that bombshell on him guaranteed to alter the terrain of his beliefs. And then left him alone to assess the damage.

There'd been plenty.

Quinn had stayed by the fire until the embers faded from red to gray. When he finally walked back to his cabin, he saw the sliver of light shining under the eaves where Abby's bedroom was located. Did Abby have a difficult time falling asleep, too? If the coffee tasted as strong as it smelled, it was a good indication that she had.

He tapped on the screen door.

"Come in." Abby's voice floated down the stairs. The official lilting cadence of a morning person. "I'll be right down. Pour yourself a cup of coffee."

Quinn made his way to the kitchen and stared in disbelief at the array of baked goods on the table. The inn hadn't opened and it looked as if Abby were already cooking for a dozen people.

"Have a..." Abby came around the corner as he was reaching for a sample. She smiled. "Cinnamon roll."

Quinn's mouth went dry.

He'd teased Abby the day before about her resemblance to Huckleberry Finn. This morning, she was the woman on the billboard for Porter Hotels.

The white sundress Abby wore made her sun-kissed skin appear even more golden. Pencil-thin heels replaced the plastic daisy sandals. Her hair was subdued in a neat coil at the nape of her neck, showcasing a diamond cross necklace and matching earrings. The stones weren't large or gaudy but they glowed with a soft fire that told Quinn they were genuine.

If it hadn't been for the familiar, luminous smile, Quinn might not have recognized her.

"Are you bringing a mid-sermon snack?" He dragged his gaze away.

She smiled. Call him an idiot, but he couldn't get enough

of Abby's smile. "This is my contribution for the potluck after the service."

"There's a potluck?"

"Mmm." Abby tilted her head. "I thought I mentioned that."

"No. You didn't." Quinn's plan to arrive late and leave early began to unravel.

"Don't worry about bringing something. I have enough for both of us."

That wasn't what Quinn was worried about. He was worried about spending more time than absolutely necessary under the scrutiny of the people who attended Church of the Pines. He was used to people talking about him; he didn't want to cast a shadow on Abby's reputation.

She poured two cups of coffee and handed him one. "Have two cinnamon rolls if you'd like. We're celebrating."

"Celebrating?"

"Last night when I came in, there was a message on the answering machine from a woman named Lydia Thomas. She and her husband are missionaries in the Philippines, but they're here on furlough for the summer. Apparently, her cousin lives in Mirror Lake and mentioned that I was opening a B&B here." Abby paused to take a breath. "She and her husband, Simon, met and fell in love when they were camp counselors one summer. They'll be celebrating their fiftieth wedding anniversary and they want to renew their vows. *Here.*"

"Your first guests." Quinn thought of all the work that still needed to be accomplished but didn't want to dampen her excitement.

"That's not all." Abby's eyes shone as bright as the diamonds around her neck. "They want to rent out all five cabins so they can invite their friends and family to witness the vow renewal—in the chapel." Abby performed a graceful ballerina twirl, the filmy skirt of her dress swirling around her knees. And, Quinn couldn't help but notice, she did it without spilling a drop of coffee. "Can you believe it? The chapel, Quinn! That's where her husband proposed."

The dreamy look on her face told Quinn that she was caught up in the romance of it all. His thoughts took a more practical turn.

All five cabins. He did some quick calculating in his head. Three of them were finished. Installing new locks and a security system would take up the bulk of his time the first part of the week but it was possible he could have another cabin done by the time Daniel returned.

"Which weekend are they going to reserve?"

Abby bit her lip. "That's the tricky part."

"The *tricky* part?" Quinn's stomach contracted. "Don't tell me they want to rent out the place the weekend of your grand opening?"

He remembered her mentioning that she hadn't taken any reservations yet because she initially planned to rely on word of mouth rather than formal advertising. The grand opening was supposed to provide people with an opportunity to tour the grounds, view the rooms and sample some of the food Abby planned to prepare. If she took in guests that weekend, visitors wouldn't have the freedom to explore.

"No. They're scheduled to go back to the Philippines. Lydia wanted to know if there was any way I can accommodate them the weekend before."

It took a moment for her words to sink in. "They want you to open the inn a week *early?*"

"Yes."

Amazingly, a sparkle danced in Abby's eyes instead of the panic Quinn should have seen there.

"What did you tell her?"

"Nothing yet. It was too late to return her call last night but I plan to call her back right after church."

"To tell her no, right?"

"You should have heard Lydia's voice, Quinn. She sounded thrilled at the idea of renewing their vows in the chapel where Simon proposed to her."

Lydia and Simon.

Abby had never met the couple but the warmth in her tone made it sound as if she'd known them forever.

"That's two weekends from now." Someone had to be the voice of reason and Quinn figured since he was the only other person in the room, the task fell to him. "You aren't even sure you'll have things ready in time for the grand opening."

The voice of reason, however, didn't put a dent in Abby's enthusiasm.

"I prayed about this a lot during the night and I really think it's what I'm supposed to do," Abby said. "Lydia and Simon have spent fifty years together on the mission field. If I can do something special for them, I'm trusting that God will give me the means to accomplish it."

The closer they got to church, the quieter Quinn became.

Not, Abby thought, that he'd been Mr. Talkative since she'd told him about the Thomases' vow renewal. He hadn't argued with her decision but she could tell he wasn't happy with it, either.

But, she reminded herself, he hadn't heard Lydia's voice on the answering machine. The woman had sounded as breathless and giddy as the seventeen-year-old girl who'd fallen in love that summer over fifty years ago.

How could she say no?

There was no denying, however, that it would take a tremendous amount of time and energy to have the inn ready for guests a full seven days earlier than Abby had originally planned. Not to mention the food preparation. Lydia had asked if she would consider catering a small reception after the vow renewal.

She hadn't told Quinn that. He already thought she was crazy for even *thinking* about opening the inn early. Fortunately, he'd let the subject drop after she'd reminded him that she believed in God's plans and purposes, not coincidences.

You'll have to help me, Lord. There is no way I can do this without You.

"Are you coming?"

With a start, Abby realized they were in the parking lot.

"Sorry." She slipped out of the car and smoothed the wrinkles from her skirt. "I was thinking about Lydia and Simon Thomas."

"How you hate to disappoint them this time around but you would love to see them the next time they're in the States?"

"No." Abby swatted Quinn's arm with her purse.

And heard a polite cough.

She glanced up and saw Pastor Wilde standing several feet away, watching them with interest.

The first time she attended Church of the Pines, she'd been a little shocked to see a handsome man in his early thirties take the pulpit at the beginning of the service. It suddenly made sense to Abby why every single woman between the age of eighteen and eighty crowded the front pews, which were typically the last to fill up on a Sunday morning.

According to Kate Nichols, Pastor Wilde came to Mirror Lake to serve as a temporary interim pastor the summer before but had stayed on when the elders, impressed by his easygoing personality and passion for the Lord, offered him the full-time position.

"Pastor Wilde." Abby felt Quinn freeze beside her. She linked her arm through his, took a step forward and felt instant resistance. "Good morning."

"Morning, Abby." The pastor smiled at her before his gaze slid to Quinn. He extended his hand. "I don't believe we've met. I'm Matthew Wilde."

Just when Abby began to wonder if she had to step on Quinn's toe to get him to make a noise, he shook the pastor's hand. "Quinn O'Halloran."

"I'm glad you're joining us today."

Quinn's chin jerked once in acknowledgment.

Abby couldn't understand his response. If he'd attended Church of the Pines in the past, why did he seem so uncomfortable?

"You asked for prayer last week." Pastor Wilde looked at her. "How are things going out at your place?"

Abby smiled up at Quinn. "Actually, my prayers were answered. Quinn came to my rescue. He took Daniel's place and he's already finished one of the cabins."

"Only two more to go," Quinn muttered.

"God does care about the details." Pastor Wilde's gaze bounced between the two of them. "I hope you're both staying for the potluck after the service."

"Oh, that's right. I almost forgot the salad. It has to be re-frigerated." Abby turned and dove into the backseat to retrieve it.

So much for Quinn's hope that he and Abby would arrive late and avoid the pre-service meet and greet. But then again, he'd also hoped to avoid the pastor and yet here he was, making nice with the guy in the parking lot.

Pastor Tracey must have retired. That shouldn't have surprised him. For all Quinn knew, the church could have seen several ministers come and go over the past fifteen years.

He hadn't missed the appreciative look in Matthew Wilde's eyes when he greeted Abby. Not that Quinn could blame him. Abby's smile gave the sun a run for its money. The pastor hadn't ogled her in an inappropriate way but it still bugged him. Quinn took a perverse satisfaction in knowing that Abby hadn't seemed to notice.

"Quinn used to attend here a long time ago." Abby returned, a large covered bowl in her hands. A strand of hair worked its way out of the pins and dropped to her shoulder like a silky yo-yo. "Now where did that come from?" she grumbled.

Without thinking, Quinn reached out and tucked it back into place.

The pastor's eyes narrowed. Like a shepherd who had just spotted a wolf stalking one of his lambs.

Stupid, stupid, stupid, Quinn silently berated himself. *Not exactly the way to fly under the guy's radar, O'Halloran.*

Abby unwittingly came to his rescue. "I suppose we should go inside. The service can't start if we keep the pastor standing out in the parking lot."

"I can take this." Quinn reached for the bowl and Abby handed it to him with one of her signature bright smiles.

"Thank you."

Matthew Wilde gave him a measured look as he picked up the thread of conversation again. "I've been trying to get to know everyone in the congregation, but I don't remember seeing your name on the membership roster."

"Like Abby said. It was a long time ago. I was in fourth grade."

"Then you're originally from the area?"

The pastor's casual tone didn't fool Quinn a bit. There

might be not a bright light shining in his face, but he was definitely in the hot seat. "Born and raised. I left after graduation."

"Where did you go?"

Abby darted a look in his direction as they began to walk toward the doors. It was clear she was as interested in his answer as the pastor was. "The marines," he said reluctantly.

"Four years?"

Quinn nodded and quickened his pace. If he was lucky, he'd make it to the man handing out bulletins before the next question.

An elderly woman bustled up to them, running interference as she planted her tiny frame in front of the pastor. Quinn would have hugged her, except he was afraid the ushers would think he was going for her purse.

Quinn took a bulletin, ignored the usher's bulging eyes as he recognized him and started down the aisle.

Only to face another complication.

The only empty pews were close to the front of the church. Which meant he and Abby had to walk up the center aisle—in front of everyone—to find a place to sit.

Abby, who seemed oblivious to the curious looks they were receiving, waved to Kate Nichols, who promptly shifted everyone over to create enough space for them for join her.

The two women, who couldn't have known each other for more than a few weeks, hugged as if they were lifelong friends. Over Abby's shoulder, Kate winked at him. The brat.

She knew he avoided her café and she knew why. He refused to provide more grist for the rumor mill.

"Hi, Quinn."

"Kate."

A smile danced in her eyes at his less than enthusiastic reply. "It's good to see you."

Quinn was saved from having to respond when a woman joined the pianist and began to sing.

As the words of the praise song flowed through the sanctuary, Quinn felt as if he were transported back in time.

The church, like the town, hadn't changed in the past fifteen years.

Sunlight streamed through the stained glass windows, painting the floor with swashes of crimson, emerald and gold. While other churches sought to modernize with comfortable chairs and PowerPoint displays, Church of the Pines remained the same.

Quinn hadn't expected to find comfort in that.

"Quinn?" Abby touched his hand.

With a start, he realized the congregation was rising to their feet to join together in the last verse of the song.

He didn't know the words but was content to listen to Abby sing them in her clear contralto.

When the song ended and they'd taken their seats again, Matthew Wilde stepped up to the front.

"Good morning, everyone." His smile swept over the congregation. "Welcome to the Church of the Pines. For those of you who are guests, I'm Pastor Matthew Wilde. And today, we're going to a place called Gilgal."

Chapter Fifteen

Quinn studied the fresh flowers on the piano. The young mother discreetly doling out animal crackers to her children in the next row. Counted the number of candles on the altar.

He even tried to come up with a way to convince Abby to tell Lydia Thomas they couldn't hold their vow renewal at the inn. But in spite of his best efforts, like the bluegill Cody had hooked and played until it finally gave up, Matt Wilde's sermon slowly began to reel him in.

"Do you know what was between the wilderness and the Promised Land?" Matt paused. "Well, if a person checked out the Scriptures, they might say it was the Jordan River. And they'd be right." He smiled. "But I think I'm right, too, when I say it wasn't only the river, it was faith.

"The Israelites, children of the Promise, had been wandering in the desert for forty years. I don't know about you, but I've done my share of wandering—even after I trusted Christ as my Savior. Like they did, I had a habit of looking back instead of forward. Sound familiar?"

Quinn saw heads begin to nod. Abby's was one of them.

"Joshua wanted to lead the people to the Promised Land,

but in order to do that, they had to take that first step of believing God and trusting Him. The water didn't part before they stepped in. It parted *after* their toes touched the water.

"Even though life in the wilderness is barren and difficult, there are times we are tempted to stay there. We start to set up camp like it's our home." Matt lifted his hands. "This is it. This is all I can expect from myself. All I can expect from God. But it isn't our true home. It's not the place we're *supposed* to dwell. God wants us to cross over into all that He has for us, not live in defeat, wandering in the wilderness.

"He had an amazing plan for His people. A plan they discovered when they stopped wandering and started trusting. The word *Gilgal* means circle. God gave the people a do-over, in a sense. Brought them full circle. The reason they'd spent forty years in the desert was because they'd disobeyed Him, but He gave them another opportunity to trust Him. He'll do the same for you. I know, because He did it for me.

"My question for you today is this, are you going to trust Him? Are you going to take that step of faith and believe His promises? You don't have to stay in the wilderness. God has something special waiting for you, too. Be brave. Take that first step of faith and find out what it is."

Instead of rising with fire and brimstone intensity, Pastor Wilde's voice dropped. To Quinn, it had more of an impact than if he'd shouted the words.

"Will you pray with me?"

Quinn automatically bowed his head with everyone else, but his thoughts were scattered in a dozen different directions...and then he felt Abby take hold of his hand.

"You aren't getting a root canal, you know." Abby tugged on Quinn's arm but it was like trying to move a mountain.

Quinn didn't budge. He noticed the pastor had finished praying.

Abby sighed and closed her eyes.

"What are you doing?"

"Shh. I'm praying for you."

"For me?" He sounded as if he were choking.

Abby nodded but didn't open her eyes. "Jesus said if we have faith like a mustard seed, we can move a mountain. Compared to that, moving you to the fellowship hall should be a piece of cake."

She peeked up at Quinn through her lashes and saw his lips tilt.

"Come on," he growled. "I suppose if we don't get in line, the only thing left will be those salads made out of Jell-O and cottage cheese."

"I always go to the dessert table first," Abby whispered.

"Lead the way." Quinn's smile kicked up another notch and Abby caught her breath.

She saw a few curious looks as they made their way to the buffet table but most of the people smiled. At both her and Quinn. Still, she could feel the tension emanating from him. As if he were expecting a lightning bolt to find him at any moment. Or someone to shoulder their way through the crowd and tell him that he didn't belong here.

Quinn hadn't commented on Pastor Wilde's sermon but she knew it had to have moved him.

Listening to Matthew's message, Abby had prayed that God would speak to Quinn. Touch his heart. The words the pastor had spoken were like a benediction to the conversation she and Quinn had had the night before.

When Quinn talked about his father, underneath the bitterness was regret. And underneath the regret, grief. The emotions layered below the surface like striations in a rock.

It was important to her that Quinn take the step of faith that would set him free from the past…because Quinn was important to her.

Abby swallowed hard as the truth washed over her.

She'd known him less than a week and yet every conversation they'd had, every smile they shared, every moment they spent together acted like invisible threads knitting her heart to his.

She had no idea if he felt the same way. But it had to mean something that Quinn had confided in her about his childhood. Sat with her by the campfire. Brought her to church…

"Can't decide?" Quinn whispered. "Take one of each. That's what I'm going to do."

Abby blinked. If she could stand in front of a table laden with mouthwatering desserts and not see them, she was in worse shape than she thought!

"I'm glad you haven't left yet, Abby." Kate rushed up to her. "There's someone I want you to meet and don't you dare slink away, Quinn O'Halloran," she added in the same breath. "Pastor Wilde is looking for you."

Before Abby knew it, Kate had whisked her away. She glanced over her shoulder and saw Quinn book-ended by Pastor Wilde and a tall, dark-haired man she didn't recognize.

"You asked me about local artists when you were at the café a few days ago," Kate said. "I don't know why I didn't think about Emma Barlow. You're practically neighbors. She lives on Stony Ridge Road about a mile away from you."

"She's an artist?"

"Emma probably wouldn't call herself that," Kate said with a low laugh. "She considers what she does a hobby, although I disagree. She has a gift. I talked her into selling three of her mosaic garden stones to me last summer and each one is a work of art. They're absolutely beautiful."

Abby could already picture a path made up of one-of-a-kind stones winding through the kitchen garden she had designed. "I'd love to meet her."

"She's right over there." Kate pointed to a slender woman sitting at a table in the corner. Her sandy brown hair and delicate features matched those of the boy sitting next to her. Brother and sister? Abby wondered. Emma looked too young to have a child that age.

The woman rose to her feet as they approached.

"Emma, this is Abby Porter. Abby, Emma Barlow and her son, Jeremy."

"Please, sit down," Emma said. "Jeremy and I are almost finished."

"Oh, we don't want your table," Kate said cheerfully. "We want you. Abby is opening a bed-and-breakfast on Mirror Lake and she's interested in buying from local artists."

Emma gave Kate a look. "I hardly qualify as a local artist," she protested.

"Don't be so modest." Kate pulled out a chair for Abby and plunked down into the one beside it. "I was telling her about the mosaic work you do."

The color in Emma's cheeks matched the carnation-pink blouse she wore. "It's just something I do in my spare time," she murmured. "To relax."

"They are good, Mom," the boy piped up. "Maybe if you start selling some of them, I can get a new bike."

"Jeremy Barlow!" Emma looked as if she wished the floor would open up and swallow her.

"Sorry." Jeremy grinned. "But it's true."

Abby took pity on her. "I'm sorry about the ambush," she said. "But I really would like to see some of your work."

"It's not…" Emma paused and the indecision in her wide blue eyes collided with Kate's scowl across the table. "I suppose that would be all right. For you to look at it, I mean."

Something in Emma's expression told Abby that even though she was giving in, she didn't want her to purchase anything out of a sense of obligation.

"Great." Abby pushed away from the table. Not only because she didn't want to give Emma an opportunity to change her mind, but because she wanted to check on Quinn.

Maybe it had been her imagination, but she had felt some strange vibes between him and Pastor Wilde in the parking lot. Abby trusted that Matthew wouldn't say or do anything to make a visitor uncomfortable, but Quinn might not perceive it that way. Judging from what he'd told her the night before, he didn't think anyone would see him as anything other than the offspring of Mike O'Halloran.

Was it possible that Quinn believed God felt the same way?

"Earth to Abby." Kate snapped her fingers a few inches from Abby's nose.

"I'm sorry." Now it was Abby's turn to blush. "I was…somewhere else."

"I'm sure you were," Kate teased. "And I should probably take you back there, or he's going to think you've been kidnapped."

Abby managed a wan smile. Knowing it was just an expression didn't prevent the knot that formed in her stomach.

She reminded herself that she wasn't wandering aimlessly in the wilderness anymore, tangled in the thorns of painful memories. Like Pastor Wilde, she had taken that step of faith into a land of abundant living that God promised.

"Mom?" Jeremy's face lit up as he turned toward his mother. "It looks like some of the guys are going to play baseball. Can I go, too?"

Emma shook her head. "We're going to be leaving soon."

Instead of arguing, Jeremy slumped lower in the chair and bulldozed a forkful of corn into what was left of his mashed potatoes.

Kate looked as if she were about to say something but changed her mind. An awkward silence descended.

"I'll call you, Emma," Abby said. "Is your number in the book?"

Emma averted her gaze. "It's listed under Joseph Barlow."

Abby hadn't missed the shadow that skimmed the surface of the other woman's eyes. If she wasn't mistaken, Emma Barlow had spent some time in the wilderness, too.

To her credit, Kate didn't say a word about Emma as they left to find Quinn. Abby was relieved. Quinn thought the Grapevine Café lived up to its name, but Kate didn't seem like the type of person who considered gossip an acceptable form of conversation.

"I don't see Quinn."

Kate chuckled. "He's a big boy. I'm sure he's still with Pastor Wilde."

Or else, Abby thought, he'd left her stranded at the church potluck.

Her suspicion increased after they took another lap around the fellowship hall. There was no sign of Quinn anywhere. Or Pastor Wilde, for that matter.

"Let's check outside," Kate suggested. "We have picnic tables set up in the yard and a lot of people take their food out there when the weather is nice."

Abby had a hard time not charging ahead of her friend as

they made their way back upstairs and out the double doors into the sunshine. Kate was right. At least half the congregation had gone outside. The older members of the congregation balanced paper plates in their hands while they chatted with friends and the younger ones sprawled on their stomachs in the grassy area off the parking lot.

"See, there he is… Oh, no."

"What?" Abby's gaze bounced from the group of boys playing touch football in the grassy field adjacent to the church to a circle of young mothers with babies in their arms and toddlers attached to their skirts like barnacles.

She couldn't see Quinn anywhere.

"I think you've been replaced."

"Replaced?" Abby frowned.

Kate pointed to a path of asphalt near the corner of the building, where a line of giggling little girls had formed, each waiting to take a turn.

Pastor Wilde held one end of the bright pink jump rope.

Quinn held the other.

Abby watched in fascination as an adorable little girl, with ink-black hair and skin a soft shade of caramel, tugged on the hem of Quinn's shirt. He continued to turn the rope with one hand and scooped her up with the other, settling her onto his hip.

Kate looped an arm around Abby's shoulders and gave them a squeeze.

"And you were worried Quinn wouldn't make friends."

Chapter Sixteen

He wasn't Superman.

Who was he kidding?

He couldn't even claim to be a real carpenter, although at least Quinn knew one end of the hammer from the other.

Not that his thumb would agree. It was still throbbing in response to being mashed a time or two. Okay, maybe more like a dozen.

It was Abby's fault he was so distracted. Thoughts of her created a hazardous work environment. Quinn was tempted to call OSHA and turn her in. Maybe that would stop her from carrying out her crazy plan to open the inn early.

On second thought, he doubted it.

Raking a hand through his hair, Quinn stepped back to survey the porch rail.

If he didn't finish soon, he'd be working in the rain. An ominous bank of clouds had unrolled on the horizon, blocking out the sun and kicking up a breeze that curled the tops of the waves that slapped the shoreline.

As soon as he and Abby had gotten back to the inn, he'd

started working on the next cabin. If she was serious about opening up a week early for the Thomases, he couldn't afford the luxury of a "rest and refresh" day.

Abby must have come to the same conclusion. She'd disappeared inside the house right after church and he hadn't seen her the rest of the day.

Quinn was hoping that once she took off her rose-colored glasses and acknowledged the staggering amount of work left to be done, she would admit defeat.

Like you did?

The mocking question rerouted Quinn's thoughts to the conversation they'd had the night before, where it dovetailed with the sermon Pastor Wilde had delivered that morning.

Like a two-by-four to his thick skull.

No coincidences, Abby said.

Quinn was starting to think that God did have a plan. And a sense of humor.

When Matthew Wilde had suggested they "take a walk and get to know each other," Quinn braced himself for part two of the interrogation the pastor had started in the parking lot.

Quinn had been a little shocked when the pastor started to talk about himself instead. And he wasn't sure how, but not only had he gotten roped—literally—into playing with a group of giggling little girls, he had also agreed to meet Matthew for breakfast on Thursday morning. At the Grapevine Café, no less.

He was about to pick up the hammer again when Lady planted herself at his feet and barked, a polite reminder it was time for her supper.

"Got it." Quinn bent down to ruffle his pet's silky ears. "Where's your sidekick?" He looked around for Mulligan. The two dogs had become inseparable during the week.

As if she understood the question, Lady looked toward the house and whined.

Quinn's eyes narrowed.

It wouldn't hurt to check on Abby and make sure she wasn't working too hard. And snag another one of her killer cinnamon rolls at the same time.

If Abby insisted on feeding him like this, he'd have to put in a few more hours of work every day to burn the extra calories off.

Not that there was a lack of work to find.

Lady followed him over to the cabin and Quinn filled her dish, shutting the door quietly behind him before making his way to Abby's.

Mulligan must have realized his buddy was missing, because when Quinn stepped onto Abby's porch, the dog's howl drifted through the open windows.

Usually Abby had praise music blasting while she worked, but other than Mulligan's mournful song, everything was quiet.

"Abby?" He opened the door and stuck his head inside.

No response.

Frowning, Quinn took a step into the foyer. The tangy odor of lemon cleaner stung his eyes.

Abby definitely hadn't been lounging around all day with her nose in a book. He could practically see his reflection in the floor.

"Abby? Are you in here?"

Mulligan heard his voice and dashed around the corner, all four paws scrambling for purchase on the glossy hardwood floor. The momentum sent him skidding toward Quinn like a baseball player sliding into home plate.

Quinn caught the dog before he took out a lamp.

The commotion didn't lure Abby to the great room. Quinn

felt the blood thicken in his veins as he made a sweep of the first floor and then the second.

He took the narrow staircase leading up to the third floor and found his path blocked by a bright green door.

Had she decided to take a nap?

"Abby?" He tapped his knuckles against the wood and turned the knob at the same time. The door swung open.

Quinn had a split second to take in the neat but tiny living quarters—pale green walls, an antique wardrobe and the sleigh bed covered in a simple patchwork quilt—before something else registered.

The bed was empty.

Now what?

There was nowhere else to look. And there was no sign of Abby. Anywhere.

Abby untied the lightweight sweater she'd knotted around her shoulders and pushed her arms through the sleeves to cloak the goose bumps rising on her skin.

The morning had started out hot and muggy, but the temperature had dropped over the past hour as a front moved in, making Abby question her decision to take a walk so close to sunset.

But scrubbing and waxing the floors for the better part of the afternoon had given her plenty of time to formulate ideas on how to decorate the chapel for Lydia and Simon's vow renewal.

Talking with Lydia on the phone had affirmed she was doing the right thing. Abby had felt an instant rapport with the elderly woman as they discussed the arrangements.

Following the old adage about honesty being the best policy, Abby explained to Lydia that the inn wasn't officially open for business for several more weeks. When Lydia immediately began to apologize, Abby assured her that she felt blessed to be part of the anniversary celebration.

It took a few more minutes to convince Lydia that she and Simon and their guests wouldn't be an imposition—as long as the couple could overlook some minor imperfections.

Even as she'd said the word, Abby wondered if leaky roofs and rotting floors could be considered imperfections.

Not, she thought as she made her way down the trail, that Lydia would even notice. When she realized Abby was offering to open the inn early, the woman's voice had thickened as she assured her that being able to renew their vows at the chapel was all the "perfect" she needed.

Abby couldn't wait to meet the couple. And she couldn't wait to tell Quinn what Lydia had said.

Guilt shot through her as Quinn came to mind.

She hadn't seen him all day. Here she'd spouted off about setting aside Sunday to "rest and refresh" and then she'd spent every minute of it up to her elbows in lemon polish.

He must have known she wouldn't change her mind because shortly after he'd dropped her off at the house, the tap of the hammer punctuated the air. As far as she knew, he hadn't even stopped for a break.

Not that Abby had, either.

As if on cue, her stomach rumbled. Ignoring it, Abby veered off the trail and followed the worn footpath that led to the chapel just as fat droplets of rain began to fall.

The eerie stillness that had settled in the air was disrupted by a pair of crows, who sounded the alarm as she approached the stone building. Their cry was taken up by a red squirrel who shimmied up the nearest oak, perching there to act as sentry.

Abby slipped inside and let her eyes adjust to the gloom.

She was used to stopping at the chapel on her daily walk, when sunlight flooded the one-room sanctuary. Now, shadows stretched across the floor and up the walls.

A low rumble of thunder broke the silence and Abby's stomach pitched. She looked up at the ceiling.

"Lord, help me not to be afraid," she murmured. "I know You're here with me."

Instead of giving her courage, the hollow echo of her voice sent another shiver gliding through her.

Determinedly, Abby took a walk around the interior, fixing her gaze on the stained glass windows rather than the dark corners.

As she paused to run the tip of her index finger around the dusty sill, a jagged spear of lightning ripped through the clouds, opening a seam in the sky for the rain to pour through.

Abby backed away from the window. Stranded. At least until it let up a bit.

The chapel didn't have electricity and she wished she would have brought a flashlight along. Not that she'd planned on having the last hour of daylight snatched away by the bank of dark clouds that had unrolled across the sky.

The wind picked up in intensity and pushed against the door, like someone trying to shoulder their way inside. Abby's mouth went dry and she tore her gaze away from it.

"Twenty guests." She said the words out loud, trying to find some comfort in the sound of her own voice. The people would be almost shoulder to shoulder in the pews, a comfortable but cozy fit.

In her mind's eye, she could see the sides of the wooden pews decorated with fresh flowers, ivy and ribbons; candles on pedestal stands lining the front of the chapel.

Abby's gaze shifted from the pews to the narrow door

behind the altar that opened into a small storage room. When she'd first discovered it, she'd found stacks of old programs and a box of props that must have been used for skits the campers put on during the summer.

She blinked in the gloom.

It looked as if the door were open a crack.

Don't be silly, Abby scolded herself, taking a tentative step back. *It's your imagination. The way the shadows are falling makes it look like it's open....*

The inside of her mouth turned to chalk.

It *was* open.

Abby backpedaled a few more steps, her eyes riveted on the door to the storage room.

She had two choices. Head back to the house in a thunderstorm or open the door and prove to herself there was nothing on the other side.

"Don't hold on to your fear. Hold on to God."

Jessica's words cut through the storm going on inside her.

Her feet felt like waterlogged sponges as she put one foot in front of the other. The shadows had swallowed most of the natural light and the door wavered as Abby reached out a hand.

It swung open at the barest touch of her fingers and she took a tentative step inside. Her gaze swept the interior of the room and she released a ragged breath.

Empty.

Relief poured through Abby and she sagged to her knees, laughing weakly. In the past, something like this would have either paralyzed her or sent her running. This time, she'd faced it.

And she knew why.

Thank You, God.

* * *

Quinn was halfway up the trail when the beam from the flashlight flickered and died.

Not that he needed it. The constant flashes of lightning were doing a pretty good job of illuminating the way.

He stopped and worked the button a few times, just to be sure. Nothing. The temptation to turn around was strong.

If Abby had gone to the chapel, a distinct possibility since he'd found her car parked in the garage, then she was waiting out the storm there. Nice and dry.

Unlike him.

If he showed up there, soaked to the skin, she was going to think he was crazy.

And she'd be right.

A shard of lightning, too close for comfort, nicked the top of one of the pines near the lake. The ground hummed under his feet.

That did it.

Even if Abby was warm and dry, there was no way he was leaving her alone up there.

He'd barely taken another step when something hurtled against him.

Quinn staggered under the impact and his feet shot out from under him as if someone had greased the trail. He fell, taking Abby with him.

As he looked up into her eyes, something about the scenario seemed strangely familiar.

"What did I do this time?" he groaned.

"What are you doing out here?" Abby scolded, raising her voice above the shriek of the wind. "It's dangerous to be under the trees in a storm."

As if to emphasize her words, another cymbal crash sounded in the treetops.

Quinn surged to his feet and brought her with him. "Let's get back to the house before we get turned into human shish kebabs."

He kept one arm around Abby while they slipped and slid their way down the trail, locked together like a pair of amateur figure skaters until they reached the safety of the lodge.

They stumbled into the kitchen and Abby sagged against the counter, her shoulders shaking as a small lake formed at her feet.

Was she hurt? Scared?

She pushed the wet hair off her face and lifted her head.

"You're smiling again." Quinn stared at her in disbelief.

"Am I?" Abby swiped a soggy sleeve against her face and giggled. "That didn't help."

He'd just had another ten years stripped off his life and she was acting like a baby duck who'd found a warm puddle to splash around in!

"What on earth possessed you to go for a walk in a storm?" Quinn said, a little amazed he was able to talk with his back teeth clamped together.

"I had some things to do at the chapel." Abby's teeth began to chatter but she grabbed a teapot off the stove and began to fill it with water. "Do you want some t-tea?"

The perfect hostess.

Quinn felt the anger drain out of him. In two strides he was by her side. Plucked the teapot from her bluish hands.

"I want you to change into dry clothes and curl up with a fuzzy blanket and read the chapter in *Survive and Thrive in the Woods* about thunderstorms," he said softly.

Abby wasn't intimidated by his scowl. If anything, her smile brightened. "And then I'll pass it on to you. I wasn't the only one out in that storm, you know. What's your excuse?"

"I went to find you," he admitted with a growl. "Because I knew you'd skip that chapter."

A droplet of water burst and ran down her cheek. Quinn stopped it with the pad of his thumb. Of their own accord, the rest of his fingers splayed over the delicate curve of her jaw.

Leave. Now.

Quinn's brain sent out an urgent SOS to his heart. He would have enough memories to keep him awake at night without adding another one. What it would feel like to kiss Abby.

"What were you thinking anyway?" He scraped up some anger. At the moment, that emotion was safer than the other ones swirling around in his head. "You could have been hit by lightning. You could catch pneumonia—"

"Quinn?"

He barely heard her over the jackhammer of his heart.

Abby came up on her tiptoes and touched her lips to his. Smiled into his eyes.

"Thank you."

Chapter Seventeen

"Good news."

Quinn rolled over and scrubbed his eyes with the back of one hand. "Porter?" he said into the phone.

"Of course." Alex sounded irritatingly cheerful at—Quinn squinted at his watch—five o'clock in the morning.

He felt as if he'd just fallen asleep. Probably because his conscience had kept him awake most of the night.

"This better be good," Quinn muttered. "And it better not have anything to do with attaching tiny surveillance cameras to squirrels."

"You're fired."

It took a moment for the words to register. "Fired?"

"Out of a job. Let go. Terminated," Alex clarified almost cheerfully. "The police took the guy who's been harassing me into custody last night. Caught in the act of sticking a wicked-looking knife into the back tires of my Viper, by the way."

Wide-awake now, Quinn propped himself up on one elbow. "Who was it?"

There was a pause, as if Alex was surprised by the

question. "The younger brother of someone I fired about a month ago. Apparently he took issue with my decision and wanted to get revenge. He's fifteen, though. Old enough to be charged as an adult."

Alex sounded as if he wished he were able to sentence the teen himself. Quinn couldn't help but compare that to the compassion Abby had shown Cody Lang.

"You know what this means, don't you?" Alex continued. "You can pack up your tools and get back to the security business."

Pack up his tools.

A week ago, he would have already been on his way back to Mirror Lake. But a week ago, he hadn't known Abby.

"Great." Quinn winced at his own lack of enthusiasm as he turned away from the sunlight streaming through the window.

He thought of all the work that needed to be done in the next two weeks so that Abby would have the inn ready for the Thomases' anniversary celebration.

"What kind of strings are you going to have to pull to get Daniel to come back early?"

Silence. And then, "I'll think of something."

Something in Alex's tone made Quinn wonder if he had another plan in mind. A prickle of unease skated down his spine.

"Daniel is going to come back, isn't he?" he pressed. "Abby won't have the inn ready in time if he doesn't."

"Really?" Alex didn't sound surprised. "I warned her she was taking on too much."

Everything clicked into place and Quinn's frustration swelled. "You're a master at pulling strings but you aren't going to get Daniel to come back, are you? You *want* Abby to fail."

"I want her to come to her senses," Alex retorted. "I told you that she's fragile. It's my job to protect her."

"Fragile?" Quinn repeated. "Abby is one of the strongest people I know. She's been putting everything she has into this place. And it isn't your job to undermine her decisions. It's your job to support them."

"You don't understand what my job is. It's not that I don't support her decisions. It's this particular decision. Abby doesn't have what it takes to run a bed-and-breakfast. I want her to realize that before she gets in over her head."

Were they talking about the same person here?

Quinn's frustration propelled him out of bed and he stalked to the window. "I think you're underestimating her. Quit playing the protective big brother card. If you loved her, you'd be spending your time and energy helping her get this place into shape, not trying to think of ways to get her back to Chicago." Quinn didn't bother to sugarcoat it. It wasn't as if Porter could fire him twice.

"You don't know anything about my family. And you've only known Abby a week. You don't know anything about..."

"About what?"

"Her past."

"She told me about your parents. I realize that you feel responsible—"

"I'm not talking about that," Alex said tightly.

"Then what are you talking about? You got me into this. I think you owe me an explanation."

"Fine." Alex snapped the word. "Maybe if I do, you'll understand where I'm coming from. Abby was abducted by a hotel employee when she was six years old."

The air emptied out of Quinn's lungs.

Abducted.

A dozen possible scenarios played out in his mind and every one of them added to the weight on his chest. "What happened?"

"My parents fired Sid after they caught him stealing. He bet on the horses. Had gambling debts that needed to be paid. The thing was, if he would have asked instead of taking the money, my dad would have helped him out."

"He asked for a ransom."

"No. He lured her away out of revenge. To prove to my parents that they weren't untouchable. That bad things could happen to them, too. It took the police almost two days to find Abby. I was only thirteen at the time, but I remember the look on our parents' faces when they found out she was missing. I think it was the first time they realized success comes at a price."

Alex's soft laugh, stripped of humor, hinted that he was under no such illusion. "Things changed in our family after that. No more open door policy at the hotels. No more treating the employees like family. They enrolled us in private schools. Mom and Dad couldn't undo the past, but they did everything to make sure something like that would never happen again."

They'd closed ranks, with Abby in the middle.

"Dad took me aside one day and told me that it was up to us to do everything we could to make sure nothing like that ever happened again."

Alex had taken it to heart. Abby had been a teenager when their parents died, leaving her brother to carry that burden alone. No wonder he'd lost it when someone had started to harass him.

Quinn wondered if the Porters' attempt to shield Abby from further harm had done just the opposite. They'd insulated her in an attempt to ease her fears—but Abby had been a child at the time. What if their actions had only served to affirm there was a reason to be afraid? A reason not to trust people.

He let out a slow breath. It hurt. "Does she remember?"

"Enough to cause a mild panic attack on occasion. She described it to me once. Sometimes they're triggered when there are a lot of people around or someone she doesn't know gets too close to her. She doesn't trust easily. I've seen her at a party, laughing and having fun, and the next minute she leaves. Just like that. Now do you understand? Can you imagine her running a bed-and-breakfast? Strangers showing up at her door night and day. Living in the same house with her. It isn't a good fit."

Quinn plowed a hand through his hair and inadvertently touched a sensitive spot on the back of his neck. The place where his head had connected with the floor of the chapel the week before.

The first time he'd met her, she did seem uncomfortable when he got too close to her. And hadn't he questioned Abby's strong reaction when he'd surprised her that day in the chapel?

Not that this was the answer he'd wanted to hear.

"You've seen it, haven't you?" Alex asked quietly. "You know what I'm talking about."

Quinn had seen it. But he'd also seen other things. He'd seen Abby put aside her own misgivings and give a troubled boy a chance to prove himself. He'd seen her giving one hundred and ten percent to a business that would showcase her gifts and talents...and challenge her deepest fears.

He'd seen her faith.

"Believe me," Alex continued. "This is what's best for Abby. If she puts all this time and effort into the bed-and-breakfast and then realizes she can't do it, she's going to feel worse than if she hadn't tried it at all."

A movement caught Quinn's eye. Abby and Mulligan were walking down to the lake. Given the fact that Abby had another long day ahead of her, there shouldn't have been a bounce in her step. But there was.

In spite of all the obstacles, she believed God had brought her to Mirror Lake. Abby was doing exactly what Pastor Wilde had encouraged the congregation to do. To step forward in faith.

"I think you're wrong," he heard himself say. "You should come up here and take a look at what she's done to the place. You'd be surprised."

"No offense, O'Halloran, but she isn't your problem anymore. It's over. Mission accomplished. You can get back to your own business now."

And stay out of his.

Quinn got the message, loud and clear.

So that was it. He was supposed to walk away. It's what he'd planned all along. So why did the thought twist his stomach into a knot?

Because you thought Abby would be an assignment. You never thought you'd start to care about her.

Unbidden, the memory of her impulsive, petal-soft kiss came to mind. It had taken all Quinn's self-control not to follow up with one of his own. Instead, he'd left a millisecond after he saw the dazed expression in Abby's eyes when she realized what she'd done.

"I don't have to remind you that our arrangement stays between the two of us," Alex said.

"You just did." Quinn's gaze remained riveted on Abby. She'd kicked off her sandals and waded in the shallows, arms outstretched, face tilted toward the sun.

Was her brother right? Maybe being the proprietress of a bed-and-breakfast wasn't the best career choice for someone who'd been through what Abby had. And if that were true, wouldn't it be better to accept that now? To cut her losses and close the place down before she invested even more of herself?

Alex's dry chuckle jerked him back to reality. "I have to admit, it's been interesting working with you."

Quinn didn't need one more reminder that the past few days had been a job. Keeping an eye on Abby simply a means to an end.

"By the way, don't be surprised if you get a phone call this morning."

"Jeff Gaines." The last thing Quinn wanted to think about was the condos. The bid he'd thought would solve all his problems. *Right.*

"No. From your old boss at Hamlin Security."

Quinn's fingers tightened around the phone. "What did you do?"

"You give me way too much credit, O'Halloran," Alex said dryly. "If you kept up with the news down here, you'd know that Serena Raynes checked into a private rehab facility over the weekend. Her older brother was formally charged with providing her with prescription drugs. You were right. And I'm pretty sure your old boss is going to call you and tell you that. After he swallows that mouthful of humble pie."

Quinn braced one hand against the wall and closed his eyes.

Hamlin Security might want him back. He'd spent seven years of his life there—close to a promotion when Serena's accusation had cost him his job.

"You have a chance to get your life back," Alex said. "Everything you wanted."

A week ago, Quinn thought he knew what he wanted.

Now he wasn't so sure.

"I know you miss her." Abby paused to pat Mulligan's head, sympathetic to the mournful look in his eyes. "And no, I don't know when they'll be back."

While supervising the deliverymen who'd arrived to unload the new furniture for the cabins, she'd seen Quinn put Lady in his truck and drive away.

Five hours ago.

Abby couldn't shake the feeling that something was wrong.

He'd spent the entire morning and the better part of the afternoon putting dead-bolt locks on the doors of the lodge. Abby had bribed him into stopping for a lunch break with her, but Quinn used the time together to explain a design for a security system that would warn her if a car passed a certain point in the driveway. He'd also suggested surveillance cameras so she could see who was outside the door after regular business hours.

She'd been impressed, but not surprised, at how knowledgeable he was. Quinn would make a success out of O'Halloran Security.

When she'd told him that, he hadn't looked as if she'd given him a compliment. Just the opposite.

The only reason she could find for the sudden change in his behavior was her decision to open the inn early for the Thomases' anniversary party.

Or because you kissed him.

She groaned at the reminder.

Maybe she could plead temporary insanity, because she still wasn't sure what had come over her. The gentle caress of his hand against her cheek? The velvet roughness of his voice while he lectured her about the danger of wandering around the woods in a thunderstorm?

The look of stunned surprise in his eyes after she'd kissed him remained etched in her memory. So was his response. By the time she drew another breath, the door had already closed behind him. Leaving her alone to deal with the fallout of her decision.

It was ironic, really, Abby decided now that she'd had a

chance to think about it. The woman leery of men, the woman who looked for ulterior motives and tested their sincerity, had been the one who'd thrown caution to the wind and initiated their first kiss….

First, last and only kiss, she silently amended as she peeled back a corner of the dish towel to check the bread dough.

She must have done something wrong because it remained as flat as her mood.

Maybe she should call Quinn's cell phone and find out where he was and when he planned to return…

Ack.

Abby caught herself.

"Repeat after me. You are *not* Alex."

And Quinn wouldn't have left without a good reason. More than likely, he'd gone back to his own office to work on the security system he'd designed for the inn.

She gathered up some supplies and a cookbook. "Come on, Mulligan. We miss them but it doesn't mean we should sit around and sulk all evening."

The droop of the dog's ears said that sulking was fine with him, thank you very much, but he trailed behind her as she went out the back door and headed toward the fire pit.

Thanks to Quinn's helpful suggestions, Abby had a fire going in no time.

She fed tiny sticks into the flames and waited for that familiar feeling of contentment to sweep away the restlessness in her soul. The first stars winked above her. The mournful cry of a loon drifted across the lake. It was a perfect evening…except for one thing.

Quinn wasn't with her.

A few nights ago, they'd sat together in this very spot and Quinn had told her about his father.

Abby hadn't brought it up again but she'd been asking God to speak to Quinn's heart. His bitterness over his dad's shortcomings held him captive. Until six months ago, she'd been there. Dragging that kind of chain around was hard work. Freedom, Abby knew, felt a lot better.

If only Quinn would see it…

The marshmallow on the end of the stick she was holding over a cluster of embers suddenly burst into flame. Frantically, Abby started to wave it around in an attempt to put it out.

"The Fourth of July fireworks were a few weeks ago."

Abby dropped the willow branch into the fire, marshmallow and all, as Quinn emerged from the shadows. The sight of him set off a few fireworks inside of her.

She hadn't realized until now that a tiny part of her had been afraid he wouldn't come back.

"Hi, stranger." Abby tried to keep her smile under control but failed.

"Hi." Quinn stopped several feet away and pushed his hands into his pockets.

"I was wondering what happened to you."

Quinn didn't pick up the hint. "What are you doing?"

"Making s'mores. When I was talking to Lydia, she said it was one of the things she and Simon had done together when they were camp counselors. I'm practicing so I can make them one evening while they're here. As a surprise."

"You're practicing? Making s'mores?"

"I keep burning the marshmallows. Not that Mulligan minds," she added with a laugh. "There must be a trick to it. I'm open to suggestions…"

Quinn moved closer but with obvious reluctance. Unexpected tears scorched the back of Abby's eyes and she looked away. The awkwardness between them was her fault.

Her and her impulsive kiss.

"Where is the chocolate?" He surveyed the ingredients strewn on the blanket beside her.

Abby's fingers curled around the empty foil wrapper in the pocket of her sweatshirt. "I'm practicing without chocolate."

Because she'd eaten all of it while waiting for Quinn's return.

A ghost of a smile touched his lips. "Uh-huh."

The smile gave Abby courage. She patted the blanket next to her. "Well? Are you going to help me sharpen my s'more-making skills?"

"Abby—" The rest of the sentence broke off in a sigh. Quinn didn't move but she felt his retreat. Knew what he was going to say before he said it. "I'm pretty beat tonight."

It wasn't the whole truth and Quinn could tell by the look on Abby's face that she *knew* it wasn't the whole truth.

He'd spent the last few hours driving aimlessly down pitted county roads, wondering what to do.

Praying about what to do.

He wasn't sure how, but he'd ended up back on a very familiar road.

He'd seen the relief in Abby's eyes when he and Lady had returned. Heard the question in her voice when she asked what had happened to him.

Quinn could hardly wrap his mind around it. In the course of a single day, his life had been turned upside down.

Alex Porter had fired him. Bob Hamlin wanted to meet with him.

But here he was. Back at the lodge.

Because Abby needed him.

Chapter Eighteen

Finished.

Abby stepped back to admire the new valances. The crisp blue curtains, bordered by a jaunty stripe of white grosgrain ribbon that gave them a nautical look, were the finishing touch on the cabin Lydia and Simon would be occupying during their stay.

The last two cabins were still a long way from being ready but it felt good to check this one off the list.

Quinn's personal belongings were lined up neatly by the door, waiting to be relocated to the next cabin.

Tim and Zach Davis had shown up right after breakfast. Quinn assigned one of them the task of mowing the grass and the other trimming weeds around the buildings. It was obvious from their disappointed expressions that they'd hoped Abby needed more fish.

She'd tried to cheer them up the best way she knew how. With a piece of homemade cinnamon streusel coffee cake. It seemed to work...until she'd asked about Cody.

The brothers had exchanged a look and then explained

they hadn't seen him since Quinn had dropped him off at home on Saturday evening.

Abby had tried not to let her concern for the boy show but decided to ask Quinn if there was something they could do.

If she had a chance to talk to him.

Abby had hoped if she knocked on the door of his cabin early enough, they would have a few minutes to talk. But Quinn had opened the door for her and kept right on going, muttering something about checking on Zach and Tim.

The past few days had been a whirlwind of activity but it was clear that Quinn was still avoiding her. Whenever he saw her approach, his expression turned wary. Guarded. And she lost her nerve.

Maybe he was afraid she was going to kiss him again.

The trouble was, she wanted to kiss him again. And talk to him. Laugh with him. Sit by the fire with him.

Every day that brought her closer to reaching her goal of finishing the cabins brought her one day closer to losing Quinn. Daniel was scheduled to return on Monday and Quinn would go back to O'Halloran Security.

The temptation to ask him to stay on and help her and Daniel finish the cabins for the Thomases' party was strong, but Abby knew she couldn't bring herself to put that kind of pressure on him. Quinn had more than enough work of his own to catch up on.

She had a plan, though. Quinn had given up so much of his time that Abby wanted a chance to repay him somehow. She had even gathered her courage and called Faye McAllister the day before. She suspected that having Quinn's office manager on her side would guarantee her success.

Faye was enthusiastic about the idea but warned her that Quinn had stubbornly refused any offers she'd made over the past year to spend her own money on anything related to his business. The only thing he'd allowed her to do was donate curtains for the office—and that was only because she'd put them up before she asked him for permission.

Abby wasn't worried. Under certain circumstances, she could be just as stubborn as he was. Like it or not, there were times when the Porter DNA prevailed.

She was about to leave when Quinn's cell phone began to hum on the coffee table next to her.

He'd been in such a hurry to avoid her that he must have forgotten it.

She grinned.

Here was her excuse to talk to him.

Abby swiped up the phone and automatically glanced at the tiny screen. Blinked when she saw the familiar name.

Alex Porter.

It couldn't be. Why would her brother be calling Quinn?

There was one way to find out. She flipped open the phone. "Hi, Alex."

The silence on the other end was a dead giveaway.

"Abby?"

"Don't sound so surprised. How did you get this number?"

"I—" Alex hesitated.

Alex *never* hesitated.

Her hands suddenly felt cold. "Why are you calling me on my carpenter's phone."

"O'Halloran is still working for you?"

Wait a second…

"You know Quinn?"

"Not…personally."

"Alex."

"It's not what you think."

Abby hadn't been thinking anything. Until now.

"You weren't trying to get in touch with me, were you? You called this number on purpose. To talk to Quinn."

"Ab—"

"Don't lie to me, Alex." The shrillness of her own voice made Abby wince. "How did you know about him?" A thought occurred to her. "You had a background check done on him, didn't you?"

It was the only possible explanation. She couldn't remember if she'd mentioned to Alex that someone was filling in for her carpenter temporarily but if she had, her brother would have wanted to make sure Quinn's record was clean.

"I hired him."

Abby frowned. "How could you have? He took Daniel Redstone's place…"

When Daniel mysteriously won a contest he hadn't even remembered entering.

Abby sank into the closest chair and pressed a hand against her churning stomach.

"Listen to me, Abby. I was worried about you being alone up there. Someone started harassing me a few weeks ago and when the police couldn't catch the guy, I admit that I freaked out a little. I needed to know that you were safe. That's why I hired O'Halloran."

"To watch me."

"It's not as bad as you make it sound."

No, it was worse.

The pieces began to fall into place even as Abby's heart began to fall apart.

How Quinn seemed to put aside his initial reserve and spent more time with her. Inviting himself along on her trip to town. Meeting up with her at the chapel. His insistence on going to church with her Sunday morning.

The campfire…

Tears burned the backs of Abby's eyes.

She'd been foolish enough to think of him as a friend. That he'd sought out her company because he wanted to be with her. That he was beginning to care about her. Not because Alex had paid him to.

"Why Quinn? How do you know him?"

"That isn't important."

It was to her. "You owe me an explanation." She couldn't believe her voice sounded so firm. So even.

"I recognized his name when I was looking for someone in your area who could help me out," Alex finally admitted. "Someone I could trust to be discreet."

Discreet. In other words, he needed someone willing to deceive her by pretending to be a carpenter.

"What do you mean you recognized his name?"

"He was a bodyguard for Hamlin Security in Chicago before he moved back to Mirror Lake," Alex said reluctantly. "One of their best."

"A bodyguard." A bubble of laughter burst out even as tears leaked out the corner of Abby's eyes. "Of course he was."

"Let me explain—"

"I've heard all I want to." More than she'd wanted to. But she still had to ask. "Does he know? About me?"

Alex knew what she meant. "Yes."

So not only did Quinn assume she wasn't capable of looking after herself, he felt sorry for her, too.

Abby Porter. Poor little rich girl.

"He didn't want to take the job, Abby. I didn't give him much of a choice."

As if that somehow made it okay.

"Goodbye, Alex."

"Abby, wait—"

"I've been waiting, Alex. Waiting for you to stop treating me like I'm still that traumatized six-year-old. That was one of the reasons I left Chicago. I realized that I was never going to get past what happened because you wouldn't let me." She drew a ragged breath, not sure at the moment whose betrayal hurt the most. Alex's or Quinn's.

The screen door opened and Mulligan and Lady clattered in, Quinn a step behind them. In his hands was a bouquet of Queen Anne's lace and brown-eyed Susans.

The smile on his face faded when he saw the tears tracking her cheeks.

"Abby? What is it?" He was at her side in an instant.

"It's for you."

She handed him the phone and walked out the door.

"Hello?" Quinn barked the word into the phone as he started after Abby.

"Why are you still there?"

Porter.

Quinn's feet suddenly melted to the floor. "What happened? What did you say to her?"

"She saw my name come up on your phone," Alex said. "And wondered why I was calling *her* carpenter."

"What did you tell her?"

"The truth."

The truth.

Quinn's throat closed.

"You stayed, didn't you?" Alex made it sound more like an accusation than a question. "Why? I told you that I didn't need you anymore…" His voice ebbed away and then came back stronger. "You stayed because *Abby* needed you."

"I have to talk to her." Quinn saw Abby sprint across the yard and disappear into the house.

"You need to talk to me first," Alex shot back. "Is there something going on between you and my sister?"

"No." At least, not anymore.

The stricken look in Abby's eyes flashed in Quinn's mind.

The past few days he'd been trying to find a way out of the mess he'd gotten himself into. He hadn't expected it to blow up in his face.

"I'm trying her cell from my other line. She isn't picking up." Alex's own frustration spilled out. "This wouldn't have happened if she hadn't picked up your phone. The phone that wouldn't have been there if *you* hadn't been there."

Quinn didn't bother to come to his own defense. He didn't have one. "I'll talk to her."

"She won't talk to you," Alex predicted.

He had to try anyway.

Porter had been wrong about a lot of things. Quinn prayed he was wrong about that, too.

Abby took a deep breath when she heard the front door open.

Five minutes hadn't been enough time to prepare herself to face Quinn. Not that it mattered. Abby doubted if a month would have been enough.

She stood behind the small check-in area, an antique buffet she'd converted into a counter, so there would be something solid between her and Quinn. He wouldn't be able to see her knees shake, either.

The anger she'd felt while talking to Alex had drained away, leaving her feeling numb. And incredibly stupid.

The irony of the situation had begun to sink in. In the past when a man tried to get to know her, Abby would look for ulterior motives. Signs of a hidden agenda. Quinn had been the exception. She knew she was falling in love with him. But now? Now it just felt as if she were falling.

He appeared in the doorway. Abby waited for him to say something. An excuse. An apology. An explanation. Instead, he seemed to be waiting for her to speak.

So she did.

"I want you off my property. Now." Abby was amazed her voice wasn't quivering like the rest of her. "My brother might have hired you, but I think I have the right to fire you."

"All right." Quinn nodded once. Pivoted toward the door.

He was leaving. Just like that.

"That's all you're going to say?" How could he look so calm when Abby felt as if she were bleeding to death on the inside?

Quinn paused. "Alex is worried about you. Talk to him."

From his remote expression, Quinn might as well have been a stranger standing in the doorway. Abby looked for the man whose smile had melted her heart like chocolate in the sun. The one who'd worked tirelessly from sunrise to sunset so she could open the inn on schedule…

Because Alex paid him to.

"I guess Alex was right about you." Abby tossed the words at Quinn's back as he turned to walk away. "You were the best one for the job."

Chapter Nineteen

"I haven't been stood up since fifth grade, when Tammy Higgins didn't meet me at the monkey bars during recess like she promised."

Quinn flicked an impatient glance at the man sauntering up to him. "I forgot."

Matt Wilde grinned. "I believe you. But only because you know that lying is bad."

"Tell me about it," Quinn muttered.

The pastor propped a hip against the woodpile, where Quinn had been taking out his frustration on a helpless cord of oak in the backyard.

"Maybe you should tell *me* about it."

"No, thanks."

"Why not?"

"I'm not, how do you say it? A member of your flock. Not anymore, anyway."

"If you know that expression, there's a good chance you are." Matt grinned. "So, spill your guts, O'Halloran."

Quinn speared him with a look. "Are you sure you're a minister?"

"Yes, but let's put that little detail aside for the moment and pretend I'm your friend."

Quinn winced. "You're doing this on purpose, aren't you?"

"Tell me what's going on and I'll tell you if I'm doing it on purpose."

"I don't know where to start."

"You can start by telling me why you didn't show up at the café this morning. Leaving me at Kate Nichols's mercy, by the way."

"Better you than me." Quinn picked up the ax and attacked another log. So what if it was only the end of July? Winter came early in northern Wisconsin.

Without asking, Matt picked up another ax and joined in. For a few minutes, the only sound was the dull thwack of the two axes turning logs into kindling.

"Abby Porter."

The second Matt Wilde said the name out loud, Quinn's ax missed its mark and sank into the ground.

"There." Matt's smile was smug. "I started. Now it's your turn."

"You don't give up, do you?"

"Do you?" Wilde neatly turned the tables on him.

Quinn's frustration fled, replaced by relief. "You talked to Abby."

It had been difficult enough to leave the day before. More difficult knowing that she had to sort through everything alone. The way things stood with Alex, Quinn didn't think she would talk about it with him. Her friendship with Kate Nichols probably hadn't reached the point where Abby would consider her a confidante, either. Which meant that Abby was alone.

"No." Matt denied it. "As a matter of fact, I haven't seen Abby since Sunday, when the two of you came to church together."

"Then how…" Quinn stopped when he saw the wry look on the other man's face.

"I took a guess." The pastor propped the ax against the woodpile and clipped Quinn on the shoulder. "And I was right. That means you owe me a cup of coffee."

"Well?" Quinn stopped pacing long enough to aim the question at Matt. He wasn't a pacer by nature but he'd practically worn a rut through the floors of his house over the past twenty-four hours.

After Abby ordered him off her property, he'd loaded up his things, put Lady in the truck and went home. He hadn't even made an appearance at the office to let Faye know he was officially back to work.

"Well what?"

"I stopped talking. Isn't this when you tell me everything will be all right?"

Quinn had spent the last hour telling the pastor everything that had happened. Spilling his guts, just like Matt had encouraged him to do. He'd heard that confession was good for the soul but Quinn didn't buy that anymore. If anything, saying the words out loud—telling someone what he'd done—had only made him feel worse.

Matt blew out a sigh. "I don't know that it will be. She found out that two people she cared about—two people she trusted—weren't honest with her. That's a lot to process, especially considering what Abby has been through. She needs people to encourage her to move forward, not try and hold her back."

Quinn didn't need the reminder. When his imagination wasn't tormenting him with images of Abby's expression when she'd handed him the phone, it was conjuring up pictures of her as a child, taken away from her home and family.

"Why didn't you tell Abby that you came back after her brother told you he didn't need you anymore?"

"It wouldn't have mattered." Quinn knew it was true.

Weighed against the rest of the things he'd done, why would Abby believe him if he told her the reason he'd gone back to the lodge that day?

Matt considered that. "So, what happens now?"

"You're the pastor. I was hoping you could tell me."

"Are you going to give her some time to cool down and then talk to her?"

If Matt had heard Abby's parting comment, Quinn thought, he wouldn't even ask that question. It had found its mark. Knowing he'd deserved it kept the wound from healing.

"I can't." He didn't deserve her forgiveness. It was the reason he hadn't tried to make excuses or explain that he'd agreed to Alex's terms because he'd wanted O'Halloran Security to be a success.

It was more important to him now that Abby was successful.

"Do you think her brother's concerns are valid?" Matt asked carefully.

Quinn had asked himself that same question at least a dozen times. And every time, he came up with the same answer. "No. I think some of Abby's doubts about herself, some of her fears, were actually magnified because of the way her family treated her after the abduction. She told me that God changed her. I don't know why her brother can't see it."

"Unfortunately, we see what we want to." Matt's expression clouded slightly.

"Abby wants to have the inn ready for the Thomases' anniversary party. Alex won't try to get Daniel Redstone to come back because he wants her to fail. Unless she hires a crew, which is going to be difficult around here on such short notice, she'll have to tell them it won't be ready."

"Alex might not try to get Daniel to come back early but that doesn't mean *you* can't."

Quinn stared at him, turning the idea over in his mind before rejecting it. "Daniel does great finishing work but he isn't fast. If I could clone the guy, maybe." A thought suddenly occurred to him.

"What? I see the wheels turning in there."

"Nothing. I doubt it would work."

Matt leaned back and laced his fingers behind his head. "Humor me."

"Abby goes to your church. The congregation is supposed to help each other out, right? What if a group of volunteers showed up at the lodge this weekend for a workday?"

Matt smiled. "That's a great idea. You can bring it up tonight at the leadership meeting."

"Me?"

"It's your idea."

"But that kind of stuff is in *your* job description," Quinn pointed out. And he doubted people would listen to anything he had to say.

Matt was already shaking his head. "You've been out there. You know what needs to be done. If you make the appeal, I'll take it from there."

"Fine." At the moment, Quinn would have agreed to walk up and down the sidewalk in front of the Grapevine Café holding a sign if it meant getting Abby the help she needed.

"If we get this organized, are you going to be there?" Matt asked.

"I don't have the right to set foot on her property," Quinn

said. He wouldn't blame Abby if she called Sergeant West to haul him away, either.

Abby had trusted him and he'd taken advantage of it. Of her. She'd shocked him to the core with that kiss. That was the moment he'd realized exactly what was at stake if she found out who he was and why he was there.

Everything.

He'd tried to put some distance between them over the next few days but Abby had only seen him pulling away from her, not the reason he had to.

"She doesn't know how you feel about her, does she?"

He opened his mouth to deny it, but Matt cocked an eyebrow.

Lying. Bad. Remember?

Quinn gave in. "I wasn't honest with her about anything else. Why would she believe me if I told her that?"

"You know the saying. Actions speak louder than words."

"I know. That's why she won't believe me." Quinn paused in front of the kitchen window and drummed his fingers against the sink. "I'll call Daniel and ask him if he'll come back. I'll show up at your meeting this evening, too. But I can't do anything else."

"Fair enough."

"I appreciate you coming over." Quinn stretched out his hand. Matt ignored it.

"Not so fast." The pastor pushed one of the chairs away from the table. "We talked about Abby. Now it's time to talk about you. And then, I suggest we talk to God."

The sound of a vehicle coming up the driveway sent Mulligan on a mad dash to the front door.

Abby resisted the urge to follow him.

It wasn't Quinn. She would have recognized the ragged purr of his truck.

But you wish it was.

Abby pushed the thought away. Now that she knew the truth, she understood why he'd started to avoid her after she kissed him.

After Quinn walked out the day before, Abby had plenty of time to sort through the pieces and put them together. Alex had told her that he'd pushed Quinn into accepting the job. She knew why he'd agreed. O'Halloran Security. Her brother had obviously made Quinn an offer he couldn't refuse. One that made him turn back to his former career.

As a bodyguard.

Alex had hired him to watch her and she'd unknowingly crossed a line. A professional boundary. He'd operated within the parameters of the job. In her naiveté, she hadn't.

Mulligan began to whine, and Abby could almost feel the dog's disappointment. Instead of his friend, he must have realized the vehicle belonged to Zach and Tim Davis.

When she'd talked to the boys the day before, they'd agreed to put in extra hours at the lodge whenever they were free. As much as Abby appreciated their willingness to help out, she'd already decided to call Lydia Thomas and explain that although she was still willing to provide refreshments after the vow renewal at the chapel, she wouldn't be able to host the anniversary party for the entire weekend.

Mulligan clattered into the kitchen, tail wagging, as if to question why she wasn't at the door yet to greet their company.

"I know." Abby dried off her damp hands on a towel, turned the music down and stepped onto the porch.

Zach and Tim waved a greeting. So did the four other teenage boys that bailed out the side door of the green minivan parked in her driveway. Cody Lang was one of them.

"You brought reinforcements this morning," Abby said. "That's great."

Tim grinned. "This is nothing."

Cody offered a shy smile of his own. "Yeah. We just got here first."

"First?"

Zach pointed and Abby saw the wink of sunlight striking chrome. Another car cruised down the driveway. Followed by another.

"What's going on?"

"We'll let him tell you."

"H-him?"

"Pastor Wilde," Zach said. "He told everyone to be here at eight o'clock Saturday morning. So here we are."

Abby recognized the pastor in the driver's seat of the second car. He gave her a friendly salute as he hopped out and opened the passenger door for Kate Nichols.

"Morning!" Kate waved a lime-green feather duster in Abby's direction.

"What are you doing here?"

"Reporting for duty, of course," Kate sang out.

"You don't mind a few extra hands today, do you?" Matthew asked in a low voice as a caravan of vehicles began to line the driveway.

A few extra hands? The number of people gathering on the lawn reminded her of the volunteer crews that her favorite home makeover show drew. Abby recognized some of the people from church, but others were complete strangers.

"Mind?" Abby echoed. "I can't believe it. How did you know? Why would you—" Her voice broke off when she caught sight of a familiar figure making his way through the crowd.

"Daniel!" Abby rushed up to him. "What are you doing here? You're supposed to be on vacation!"

"Fish weren't biting that great." His eyes twinkled. "'Sides that, I missed your cooking."

"Is that so." His wife, Esther, swatted Daniel's arm but gave Abby a warm smile.

By the time everyone was assembled on the lawn, Abby estimated there were fifty people who had put aside their own Saturday to-do lists to check something off hers.

Humbled by the unexpected gift, Abby didn't know what to say as the chatter subsided and everyone looked to her for direction.

"Here. Maybe this will help." With a mischievous wink, Kate presented Abby with a bright yellow ball cap with the words *I'm the Boss* embroidered on it.

"That belongs to her, you know," someone said in a stage whisper.

Abby put it on and blushed when the noisy crew began to applaud.

Matt stepped up and put a hand on her shoulder. "Let's dedicate this project—and this day—to the Lord."

Abby would have thought her tear ducts would be completely dry by now. She was wrong. While Matt prayed, the grass blurred at her feet.

This morning, she'd felt completely alone.

God had just reminded her that she wasn't.

"Amen." Matt lifted his head and turned to Abby. "Okay. Put us to work!"

With Daniel's help, Abby divided everyone into smaller work groups and put one person in charge of each project. Matt had spent a summer on a roofing crew in college, so he pulled some of the older teens from the church youth group together to help him tear shingles off the cabins.

Esther Redstone and some of the older women in the congregation took over Abby's kitchen, filling pitchers with cold drinks and making sandwiches.

As the official foreman, Abby moved from crew to crew throughout the morning, taking time to answer questions, give instructions or hand out bottled water until it was time for lunch.

She and Kate were hauling coolers to the picnic tables when Kate suddenly paused and gave a low whistle. "Who is that?"

Abby followed the direction of her friend's finger as it traced the path of the silver Viper cruising up the driveway.

Abby folded her arms across her chest.

"That," she said, "is my brother."

Chapter Twenty

❧

"Can we talk?"

Her brother sounded so uncertain that Abby hardly recognized his voice. Very un-Alex-like.

"I don't know," she murmured truthfully.

Without waiting for an invitation, Alex sat down on one of the low wooden benches by the campfire. She almost smiled. This was the brother she knew and loved.

And because Abby did love him, she handed him the stick she'd been holding, with its perfectly browned marshmallow on the end.

The last of the volunteers had left an hour ago. Abby went to the kitchen to clean up and found it in spotless condition, thanks to Esther and the rest of the seniors who belonged to the Knit Our Hearts Together ministry at Church of the Pines.

She'd needed a quiet place to regroup. To thank God for His provision.

To try not to think about Quinn.

"You wouldn't return my calls," Alex said. "I figured you couldn't ignore me if I showed up here." He examined the marshmallow suspiciously before easing it off the stick. "I guess I was wrong."

"I didn't ignore you. There was a lot going on today." Abby refused to feel guilty.

"That's one of the things I wanted to talk to you about. Where did all those people come from?" Alex sounded so mystified that Abby couldn't suppress a smile.

"They're members of the church I attend."

"I guess that explains the sermon I heard on the roof," her brother muttered.

"Pastor Wilde gave a sermon? On the roof?"

"No, this one was delivered by a little fireball who gave me a hammer and told me to, and I quote, 'make myself useful.'"

Abby choked back a laugh. "That would have been Kate Nichols."

Alex shook his head and Abby waited for him to make a disparaging comment of some kind.

She'd known it was only a matter of time until he voiced his opinion about the inn, which was one of the reasons she'd avoided him all day. Well, that coupled with the fact that she knew her brother hadn't made the six-hour drive to Mirror Lake simply because she'd refused to return his phone calls. Alex had another agenda.

He would have talked to Quinn and found out she'd asked him to leave the property. Alex knew she would be feeling discouraged. Hoped he could catch her in a moment of weakness.

And maybe he would have, if she hadn't experienced such an outpouring of generosity that morning.

"They seem like good people, Abby."

She blinked, not sure she'd heard him right.

Alex smiled. "Yes, you heard me. This place doesn't look

anything like the pictures you showed me. I have to admit I'm impressed."

"They did get a lot accomplished, didn't they?" Abby couldn't help the hint of pride that crept into her voice. The volunteers had worked together so efficiently that she hadn't had to make that phone call to Lydia Thomas after all.

"They did. But it's *you* I'm impressed with."

Abby's gaze flew to her brother's face. "Me?"

"Quinn told me that I underestimated you."

Her breath stalled. "Quinn said that?"

"When I talked with him on Monday morning." Alex's eyes narrowed, as if he were remembering the conversation. "He also said that if I loved you, I would support your dreams, not try to sabotage them."

"I can't believe…" Abby paused. "Did you say Monday?"

"That was the day I fired him."

"But…I fired him on Wednesday." Abby stared at her brother, stunned.

Monday was the day Quinn had disappeared. He hadn't told her where he was going or why. She'd been sitting by the fire, making s'mores. And then…

"He came back." Alex made the connection before she did.

"Why?" Abby pressed her hand against her mouth.

"I think we can rule out that it was because of me," Alex said wryly. "Or because he needed the money or the extra work. I think he came back because of *you*, Abby."

Some of the old doubts surfaced.

"Because he felt sorry for me."

"Because he's in love with you," Alex corrected her.

"Then why did he leave?"

"From what I know about O'Halloran? It was probably for the same reason."

* * *

"Looks like you're going somewhere."

Quinn turned toward the gravelly voice. "Hi, Daniel. Come on in."

The pleats fanning out from the corners of Daniel Redstone's eyes deepened. "I knocked. Guess you couldn't hear me with your head stuck in a suitcase."

"How did things go out at the lodge today?" It had taken all Quinn's self-control not to call Matt Wilde and ask him about the workday at the lodge. "Did anyone show up?"

"Musta been fifty people out there. I think we got most everything done, except for some odds and ends."

"Abby will be able to host the Thomases' anniversary celebration?"

"I expect so." Daniel settled his wiry frame into a cane-back rocking chair. "You accomplished a lot in the amount of time you were there. But then, you always did work circles around me. Maybe you should have been a carpenter."

"Maybe." Quinn tossed a pair of socks into the suitcase.

"Taking a vacation?"

"I don't know yet."

"Abby's brother told me you might get your old job back."

Quinn's mouth dropped open. "You know Alex Porter?"

"Not until he showed up at the lodge today. We had a nice little chat about fishing trips and being honest with people." Daniel's gold tooth flashed with his smile. "He's not bad with a hammer, either. For a city boy."

"He *helped* you?"

"Kate didn't give him much of a choice, from what I saw."

Knowing that Quinn had left and Abby was without a carpenter, Alex had probably driven up to make a last-ditch effort to convince her to return to Chicago. If the volunteers hadn't showed up, would she have agreed?

No coincidences, Abby was fond of saying. God has a plan. A purpose.

Quinn was finally accepting that as truth. He was convinced Abby was right when she claimed that God had brought her to Mirror Lake. What he wasn't sure about was where *he* fit in God's plan.

"I appreciate you coming back, Daniel." Quinn tried to stow his emotions but it wasn't as easy as it used to be.

"We help out our own, you know."

"That's good. It's important to Abby that she's part of the community."

"I was talking about you."

"Me? No." Quinn instantly rejected the notion. "I've been back for over a year and everyone still treats me like an outsider."

"You get treated like an outsider because you act like one." Daniel harrumphed. "You know folks round here. You hold yourself back and people leave you alone. You reach out a hand, there'll be someone there to grab it. You just never reached out until now. They wanted to help Abby, sure. But they went because *you* asked them. Your roots are here."

Quinn fixed his gaze on the suitcase. "What if I told you that the only reason I came back to Mirror Lake was to see what I could get for this house and Dad's business?"

"Then you would have waited until after the funeral. Truth is, you came back to stand by a man who was dying. A man who never stood by you while he was alive." Daniel cleared his throat. "That shows what kind of man you are."

"I'm no hero, Daniel."

"You hired Faye, didn't you?" Amusement danced in the other man's eyes.

A reluctant smile curved Quinn's lips. "She made me."

"You saw what no one else did. That woman was like a boat without a rudder after Doc died." Daniel smiled. "You paid off your dad's debts. Cleaned things up around the place. People had you pegged right away. They've just been biding their time, waiting for you to figure out where you fit."

Quinn tried to process what Daniel was telling him.

All this time, he'd thought people avoided him because of his last name. Daniel was implying it was because they had taken their cue from him.

Either way, it didn't matter. Not anymore. He had a meeting with Bob Hamlin in Chicago the next day.

Quinn's hands balled into fists at his side. "I can't stay in Mirror Lake."

"Because you don't want to? Or does your decision have something to do with Abby?"

"You talked to Alex," Quinn said roughly. "You know he hired me to take your place. Not as a carpenter. As a watchdog. There was no noble purpose behind it. I did it because I needed the money—and a shot at the Gaines condominium bid." Quinn almost hated to admit it. Hated to see the look of disappointment on his friend's face. "I went there under false pretenses."

"Are you afraid she won't forgive you?" Daniel's eyes met his. "Or are you afraid she will?"

Quinn felt the impact of both questions. "What are you talking about?"

"For years, I watched Mike O'Halloran sabotage his life. It was like he couldn't accept any good thing that came his way. Your mother. You. A paycheck for a job well done." Daniel's voice softened. "You say you don't want to be like your dad? Then don't let the past keep you from the future God has for you."

It sounded a lot like the sermon Matt had preached the previous Sunday.

"Did you and Matt Wilde compare notes?"

"We read the same book." Daniel smiled. "And it's full of people who stumbled and fell but they got back up again with God's help. Had the courage to go forward."

People like Abby, Quinn thought. She'd demonstrated that kind of courage when she'd moved to Mirror Lake.

"God doesn't give us one chance and then turn His back on us if we mess it up," Daniel said.

"I know." Quinn pressed his fingers against his eyes. "But I really blew it with Abby. How do I know that *she* won't?"

"You don't. That's where the courage part comes in." Daniel chuckled. "She named her dog Mulligan after all, didn't she?"

Chapter Twenty-One

"A campfire! I can't believe you thought of it, Abby!" Lydia Thomas reached out and reeled Abby in for another hug. "Doesn't this bring back memories, Simon?"

"Yes, it does. This is a real treat, Abby." Simon, a handsome man whose blue eyes hadn't lost their sparkle since the couple had arrived the day before, smiled at her. "Almost makes me feel seventeen again. We can't thank you enough for opening the inn for us early."

"He's right," Lydia chimed in. "This is the perfect end to a perfect weekend."

"You're welcome." Abby returned the smile, pleased that her attempts to recreate some of the couple's favorite experiences while they'd been camp counselors all those years ago had been so warmly received.

Within an hour of their arrival, Abby felt as if she'd known the couple forever.

Lydia and Simon's three adult children and a small contingent of grandchildren arrived shortly after they did, along with several members of the original bridal party.

Abby had given everyone a tour of the lodge and showed

them to their cabins. While they settled in, she prepared an old-fashioned cookout, serving up hamburgers and hot dogs along with potato salad and homemade vanilla ice cream for dessert.

Afterward, the older grandchildren had discovered the croquet set in the boathouse and coaxed their parents into teaching them how to play.

Any concerns Abby might have had about whether she was ready to open her home to strangers were put to rest. She loved catching a glimpse of them walking along the shoreline. Watching the kids play tag with Mulligan in the yard. And she knew it wasn't a coincidence that her first guests were a small group of people who loved her home as much as she did.

Lydia and Simon had renewed their vows earlier that afternoon and it had taken all of Abby's self-control not to break down and cry. Not only because Simon and Lydia couldn't take their eyes off each other, but because they exchanged more than vows during the ceremony. The look of love and understanding that passed between the two of them held fifty years of memories.

She'd planned the campfire as a final send-off for the family and their friends after hearing Simon mention the counselors had gathered together there every evening to recap the day's events. Lydia's blush told Abby that there was more to the story and she was hoping to find out what it was.

"This is a great fire, Abby," Simon complimented.

Thanks to Quinn, Abby thought before she caught herself. She cringed inside.

Was everything going to remind her of him? He'd only been in her life a little over a week and yet memories of him were connected to the smallest things.

"Sit with us for a while." Lydia motioned her over. "You must be exhausted."

"Are you sure?" Abby hung back. "I don't want to intrude."

"Don't be silly." Lydia scolded her in the same affectionate tone she used with her children and grandchildren. "We want you to stay."

The murmurs of agreement from the rest of the group convinced her. And Abby couldn't think of a better way to spend the evening.

"This can't be the same fire pit that was here when you and Mom worked at the camp all those years ago." Lydia and Simon's daughter, Shelly, eyed the circle of bricks skeptically.

"It sure is. I remember your mother right where you are—" Simon pointed to one of his grandsons. "And sticking her tongue out at me while I played the guitar during evening devotions."

To Abby's astonishment, Lydia didn't deny it. Instead, the woman laughed. "That's true."

"Sticking your tongue out at Grandpa doesn't sound very romantic." Eleven-year-old Lexie Thomas aimed a disapproving look at her grandmother.

Simon chuckled. "I would say it's about as romantic as the skunk she and her friends tried to chase under my cabin one night."

"Simon!" Lydia clucked her tongue. "We came here to reminisce about the good times, remember?"

"And we are." Simon winked at Abby. "We might not be here today if it weren't for that skunk."

"A skunk?" Abby looked from Simon to Lydia, trying to decide if he was kidding.

"Lydia took an instant dislike to me the moment we met." He lowered his voice to a stage whisper. "She thought I was a bit, what's the term? Full of myself."

"He was." Lydia gave her husband a fond look. "My friends and I decided to take him down a peg. There was a skunk that liked to lurk around the garbage cans near the cabins. We snitched brooms from the supply closet one evening and tried to herd it toward Simon's cabin."

From the indulgent looks the adults exchanged, it was obvious the story was a familiar one. But their children leaned forward, eager to hear the rest. So did Abby.

Simon picked up the thread of the story. "I heard a commotion and flipped the porch light on. That startled the poor little critter, but instead of running under my cabin like it was supposed to, it ran into the bushes."

"The bushes where I was hiding," Lydia added.

"Her plan, needless to say…backfired." Simon grinned.

"Literally." Lydia sighed as their grandchildren snickered. "The head counselor banished me to solitary confinement in a separate cabin for the rest of the weekend. Simon was the only one brave enough to visit me. Every night, he would show up and hand me an ice cream bar through the window. Then he would sit on the step and talk to me through the screen. He turned out to be so sweet that I started to feel guilty and finally confessed what I'd done."

"I had a confession of my own," Simon said cheerfully. "From the moment I met her, I started asking God to give me a chance to win her over. I had no idea He would use a skunk."

Everyone laughed, including Abby.

They spent a few more hours around the campfire reminiscing until Simon caught Lydia yawning and announced it was time to call it a night. The parents collected their sleepy children and drifted back to the cabins, but Abby lingered by the fire.

The time spent listening to the couple share memories of their life together was bittersweet.

It made her miss Quinn even more.

After her conversation with Alex, Abby had dared to believe that her brother was right. That Quinn shared her feelings. And when she had called Kate to thank her again for being part of the work crew, her friend confided that the workday had been Quinn's idea.

Those things had given Abby hope.

Until she discovered that Quinn had gone back to Chicago.

Alex told her how he'd lost his job with Hamlin because of Serena Raynes's accusation and remembered him saying he took over his dad's business because he didn't have a choice.

Now Quinn had been given another opportunity to decide which life he wanted to live. And he'd chosen the one that didn't include her.

Mulligan, who'd been stretched out at her feet, suddenly stood up, his gaze fixed on something in the shadows. His tail began to wag.

"Oh, no, you don't—" With all the talk about skunks, Abby wasn't going to take any chances. She made a grab for the dog's collar but he was too fast for her. "Mulligan!"

She scrambled after him, almost tripping over the rubber ball one of the Thomases' grandchildren had left in the yard.

Mulligan stopped at the edge of the shadows, looked over his shoulder at her and barked, as if waiting for her to be the brave one.

"Who is it?" She chuckled. "Friend or foe?"

"I guess you'll have to decide."

Abby's heart rolled over when Quinn stepped out of the shadows.

He'd stayed away as long as he could, but when Quinn saw the color drain from Abby's face, it made him wonder if he shouldn't have waited another day.

He'd wrapped up his business with Bob Hamlin in Chicago and made one last stop before returning to Mirror Lake. Ken

Raynes had requested a meeting with him. As part of Serena's recovery, she wanted to apologize for lying to her parents about him and had asked her father to pass on a letter she'd written to Quinn.

When Ken had asked Quinn what he planned to do, Quinn hadn't hesitated.

"I'm going home."

On the long drive back, Quinn had gone over and over what he planned to say to Abby. Which, he realized now, had only worked when he wasn't *facing* Abby.

Silence weighted the air between them. Until Abby broke it.

"I thought you went back to Chicago."

Quinn hated to see the confusion in her eyes, knowing he was to blame for it.

"I came back."

"Why?" Abby's eyes darkened. "Alex said you'd been offered your old job back. You have a chance to start over."

"I do want to start over." Quinn drew a ragged breath, knowing that what he said next would determine whether that would happen. "With you. Here, in Mirror Lake. You said you believed in second chances. I'm asking for mine."

Abby didn't say a word.

Was he getting through to her?

"I should never have agreed to work for your brother, but I told myself I had to. For the business. About twenty-four hours after we met, my loyalties changed." His expression was rueful. "I started to work for *you*. I wasn't honest before but this is the truth. I've never felt this way about anyone. You were right about God having a plan and a purpose—I was too blind to see it before. But when I picture my future, you're there. In every part of it. What can I say to make you believe that—"

"Nothing."

"Nothing?" Quinn's heart bottomed out.

Had Daniel been wrong?

Abby was so shocked to hear the husky rumble of Quinn's voice—to see him standing several feet away—that his words had barely registered.

When regret darkened his eyes, she realized Quinn had misinterpreted her silence and reached out a tentative hand to touch his face.

"I mean, you don't have to *say* anything," Abby said softly. "I believe you. Because you're here."

"*Abby.*" Quinn drew her into the warm circle of his arms and rested his chin against her hair. "I had a nice speech all prepared but when I saw you, I couldn't remember any of it. Except—" he looked down at her, his smile suddenly turning roguish "—the way it ended."

Abby wondered if there would ever come a time when that smile wouldn't send her pulse into a delighted skip.

Having witnessed the looks that still passed between Simon and Lydia Thomas, she doubted it.

Abby peeked up at him from under her lashes, a little giddy now that the barriers between them had fallen. "And how did it end?"

An answering spark flared in Quinn's eyes.

"Like this." He lowered his head and kissed her.

When they finally broke apart, the look in his silver-gray eyes stole her breath away.

"Quinn O'Halloran," she teased, her voice sounding a little breathless even to her own ears. "That felt more like a beginning."

"A beginning it is, then." Quinn's arms tightened around her. "Any objections?"

He didn't give her a chance to answer, but Abby didn't mind. She couldn't think of a single one.

* * * * *

Dear Reader,

I hope you enjoyed your first visit to Mirror Lake—a small town with a big heart.

As Quinn discovered, experiences from the past can color our perspective…and make it difficult to trust God with the future. It took Abby, who had taken that step of faith, to show him that sometimes you *can* go home again!

Watch for the second book in the Mirror Lake series, where you'll have an opportunity to say hello to old friends and meet a few new ones!

I love to hear from my readers. Stop by my Web site and say hello at www.kathrynspringer.com or write to me at Steeple Hill Love Inspired, 233 Broadway Suite 1001, New York, NY 10279.

Blessings,

Kathryn Springer

QUESTIONS FOR DISCUSSION

1. What was Quinn's perception of Mirror Lake, the town where he'd grown up? What obstacles did he have to overcome when he returned?

2. What was Abby's view of the town? How did it differ from Quinn's? Why?

3. Quinn made assumptions about Abby before they met. What were they? Were they accurate? What made him change his mind about her?

4. Why didn't Abby want to tell the people in Mirror Lake who she was? Why was it so important that she be accepted?

5. In what way did Quinn's and Abby's childhood experiences impact them as adults?

6. Sergeant West quoted the old adage, "The apple doesn't fall far from the tree," when he was talking to Abby. What do you think that means? Do you agree or disagree? Why?

7. Quinn had drifted away from God. He wasn't sure God would give him a second chance because of who he was and where he came from. What encouragement would you give someone who felt that way?

8. How did Abby's faith give her the courage to let go of her

doubts and fears? Discuss a time when you let go of your fears and held on to God.

9. What was the turning point in Abby and Quinn's relationship?

10. What did Abby do to relieve stress? What are some hobbies or activities that help you relax?

11. Alex thought he was doing what was best for Abby when he hired Quinn. What was the underlying reason for his decision? Did that make it all right? Why or why not?

12. Daniel Redstone pointed out some things to Quinn about how the people in Mirror Lake regarded him. Were they different from the way Quinn viewed himself? What impact did this have on him?

13. Have you ever had an opportunity to start over? What were the circumstances?

14. Sometimes forgiveness plays an important role in starting over. How would that be true for Abby and Quinn's relationship?

15. What was your favorite scene in the book? Why?

*When his niece unexpectedly arrives at his
Montana ranch, Jules Parrish has no idea what
to do with her—or with Olivia Rose,
the pretty teacher who brought her.
Will they be able to build a life—and family—together?*

*Here's a sneak peek of "Montana Rose"
by Cheryl St.John, one of the touching
stories in the new collection,
TO BE A MOTHER,
available April 2010
from Love Inspired Historical.*

Jules Parrish squinted from beneath his hat brim, certain the waves of heat were playing with his eyes. Two females—one a woman, the other a child—stood as he approached.

The woman walked toward him. Jules dismounted and approached her. "What are you doing here?"

The woman stopped several feet away. "Mr. Parrish?"

"Yeah, who are you?"

"I'm Olivia Rose. I was an instructor at the Hedward Girls Academy." She glanced back over her shoulder at the girl who watched them. "My young charge is Emily Sadler, the daughter of Meriel Sadler."

She had his attention now. He hadn't heard his sister's name in years. *Meriel.*

"The academy was forced to close. I thought Emily should be with family. You're the only family she has, so I brought her to you."

He took off his hat and raked his fingers through dark, wavy hair. "Lady, I spend every waking hour working horses and cows. I sleep in a one-room cabin. I don't know anything about kids—and especially not girls."

"What do you suggest?"

"I don't know. All I know is, she can't stay here."

*Will Olivia be able to change Jules's mind
and find a home for Emily—and herself?*

*Find out in
TO BE A MOTHER,
the heartwarming anthology from
Cheryl St.John and Ruth Axtell Morren,
available April 2010
only from Love Inspired Historical.*

Love Inspired

TITLES AVAILABLE NEXT MONTH

Available March 30, 2010

A MOTHER'S GIFT
Arlene James and Kathryn Springer

LOVE LESSONS
Helping Hands Homeschooling
Margaret Daley

A FATHER FOR ZACH
Lighthouse Lane
Irene Hannon

HER FOREVER FAMILY
Mae Nunn

RODEO SWEETHEART
Betsy St. Amant

THE CINDERELLA LIST
Judy Baer

LICNMBPA0310